DUE PROCESS

LYNN BURKE

A lip gloss-wearing angel, Troy Emerson rouses unexpected fantasies in Silas's mind. He's also one of the attorneys hired to keep Silas from going to prison for murder.

Having been burned before, Troy avoids arrogant playboy types like Silas Barlowe. Troy believes in honesty, black and white, but the attraction between them creates incendiary clouds of magnetic gray.

When Silas stands trial, Troy is determined to help prove his actions as self-defense, but too many suspicions shadow his thoughts.

Can Silas prove he's worthy of Troy's love, or will the jury's verdict decide their future for them?

Silas

Silas didn't give two shits he'd stabbed some douchebag to death with a butcher knife, but Boston's PD sure as fuck did.

On a Thursday afternoon, he sat in an interrogation room rather than his personal office, waiting for the questions to begin. Goosebumps rose across his skin from the chill. Having been covered in blood earlier that morning, he'd been stripped of clothing for evidence and had been allowed to dress in old gym clothes from a bag in his Mercedes' trunk.

Even though he'd made the 911 call to inform the authorities about the break-in and how he'd defended himself, he still got a luxurious ride in the back of a cruiser—cuffs and all.

While he hadn't been arrested, a body lay in a pool of blood on his sister's kitchen floor, and Silas wore a bit of the dried splatter across his face that had sprayed from the fucker's neck after the killing stab.

He'd deserved what he got—

The heavy door pulled open, and a single detective entered.

"Just a reminder that these rooms are recorded," the detective said, sitting down across from Silas, his eyes as cold as his tone. "Would you state your name for the record."

"Silas Barlowe."

"And I'm Detective Marsh who you met earlier at your sister's house." The detective spouted off the date and time before settling into silence as he looked Silas over.

Silas didn't twitch beneath the man's steady stare. He'd learned long ago to not show weakness when doing business, and he refused to see his current situation as anything outside the norm.

"Tell us what happened today."

Not allowing himself to suck oxygen into his lungs to steel his nerves, Silas launched into his tale, a firm grasp on his emotions and adrenaline-crashed body. "I went to my sister's instead of my office this morning to fix her kitchen drain. The front door opened about five minutes after she left for work, so I called out to tease her about forgetting something which she's always doing. Grace didn't answer, and heavy footsteps alerted me to the fact it wasn't my sister."

The detective leaned back in his chair, arms folded, his face blank, but Silas could tell the guy didn't believe a word of his story. He'd have one hell of a time proving otherwise though.

"I got up," Silas continued, "rounded the island to find out who the fuck was in her house, and that's when the guy entered the kitchen with a gun. I managed to grab his wrist, the gun clattered to the ground, and fists started flying. Fucker wasn't that big, but he held his own enough I feared for my life."

Silas pointed at his eye which hadn't fully swelled shut but hurt like a bitch from the fucker's granite knuckles. "So I grabbed a knife from the butcher block and stabbed him in the gut. The guy was like a raging bull—kept coming at me no matter how much I managed to slash him until we ended up on the floor. I got lucky and had a clear target at his neck, so I took the opportunity."

Not one ounce of regret lined Silas's voice, but considering what the guy had broken into his sister's house for, Silas wouldn't ever feel bad about ending his life.

"Once he quit fighting, I called 911. You know the rest."

Detective Asshole/Marsh had been the first on the scene and studied him in silence a few moments.

Silas didn't so much as twitch an eyelash.

"Now tell me the truth."

"That was the truth," Silas didn't hesitate to reply.

The detective pulled his cell from his back pocket, giving Silas a reprieve from the inquisitive stare, but Silas didn't slump, didn't let out a heavy exhale to release tension from his shoulders.

No. Silas Barlowe knew how to keep steady and portray confidence even when under fire. As the CEO of a prominent acquisitions firm and having been trained by his father—the best in the business —Silas's devious side was honed to perfection.

He sat unmoved, feigning an unaffected nature. Calm, cool, and collected in the midst of the shit he'd gotten himself into.

Wasn't the first time he'd landed in trouble. Probably wouldn't be the last. His temper sometimes overcame his better senses...

Lips in a thin line, the detective shoved his cell back into his pocket and leaned forward onto the table, arms crossing. "You're aware your sister has security cameras?"

No glint lit the detective's eyes, no excitement of having one-upped Silas.

Telling as fuck.

"Of course I'm aware," Silas replied, suppressing his smirk. "I paid for the installation. The evidence is there to prove my story."

"The footage would suggest otherwise."

Silas easily held in his snort at the bullshit line.

Detective Marsh—definitely an asshole—thought to lie and trip Silas up. Once the detective went off the straight and narrow, Silas lost his desire to be helpful.

There was only one reply he would grace the detective with. "I'd like to call my lawyer, Noah Madden of Madden Law."

Detective Marsh's already thin lips firmed, but he didn't argue or badger. The law prohibited him from doing so.

"Phone?" he snapped out, and Silas rattled off Noah's office number.

Seconds later, the door slammed behind the detective, and Silas settled in for another wait, not the least bit concerned.

Minutes ticked by, and no one entered to ask if he wanted something to drink or a blanket. Enough time lapsed that Silas quit trying to keep from shivering, and he wrapped his arms around his core. He closed his eyes, reliving every minute of the day in vivid detail—and he also went over the story he'd told, word for word in his brain.

The truth as everyone would know it.

There would be no evidence to prove otherwise.

Grace had been protected, and Silas took great satisfaction in being there yet again for his little sister. The only person on the face of the earth who loved him unconditionally. The only one he'd been able to rely on.

Ever.

He supposed a day would come when a good man would take his place in her heart, but even then, Silas would always have her back.

No matter what.

No matter when.

No matter who he needed to end.

Having done it once, he'd do it again—without a second thought.

The door handle clicked, and Silas opened his eyes.

He'd expected Noah himself, so a glance at the stranger entering the room furrowed his brow.

Five-seven at the most—a damn kid for fuck's sake—posh and freshly pressed…designer suit…pink shirt a shade too flashy. Clean-shaven square jaw like those boys on a Gucci runway…fuller upper lip that appeared bee-stung. Perfectly formed nose. Strawberry-blond hair.

And striking pale blue eyes that caught Silas's breath.

A waft of sweetness, almost feminine, swept over him as he drew near.

Silas didn't give the detective behind the young man a glance as he strode forward with assurance, a cocky tilt to his head.

The first-ever male to catch Silas's eye and a surge of adrenaline sent blood rushing to his dick. Perhaps he wasn't as hetero as he'd thought—but the kid was pretty enough Silas's dick didn't care what he hid in his pants.

"Troy Emerson." The kid stuck out his hand. Smooth. Manicured. Fucking clear polish. "I'm a new associate attorney at Madden Law."

"Where's Noah?" Silas asked, reaching to accept the offer of his hand.

"Court."

Their palms clasped, static electricity racing up Silas's arm and pulsing sudden need through him, but he remained outwardly unaffected.

Troy sucked in a quiet, quick inhale, and Silas allowed his slow smile, the flash of interest to show in his eyes to let Troy know he wasn't the only one dealing with insta-lust and blood swelling in his groin.

Silas never had a man before, hadn't once considered getting up close and personal with another dick, but he wasn't averse to Troy. Every inch of his pale skin marked up from Silas's fingertips and mouth seemed like a damn good idea. Time well spent.

Troy tugged his hand away from Silas's firm grasp and settled into the chair beside him, sending a flood of his scent up into Silas's nose.

Sweet as fucking honey.

Silas's mouth watered, his dick going hard as granite. He didn't care if Troy stood or sat to take a piss. He just wanted to yank on the slightly wavy hair atop his head, taste his lips, and drink down his whimpers while Silas ravished him.

Strikingly beautiful, Troy could easily become an obsession.

Silas hadn't been antsy to get the fuck out of there until that moment. He wanted Troy alone, to do all sorts of nasty shit to him, ethics be damned—

"Is our client being charged?" Troy asked with a firm tone, snapping Silas back to the present situation he'd created for himself.

At least the kid didn't waste time or breath and sounded as confident as his attire suggested.

Why did that fact thrill the fuck out of Silas's dick?

The detective eyed Silas, his cold stare still intact, but a twitch of his lip let Silas know he wasn't pleased. "As of right now, no," the detective finally answered the lawyer's question.

"Then he's free to go." Troy got up without hesitation.

Silas mirrored his movements and towered over the little lawyer by a good six inches. Troy could have been an elf with how willowy and gracefully he moved across the room. Hot on his heels, Silas filled his lungs, discretely tucking his interested dick in the waistband of his mesh shorts. At least his T-shirt covered the leaking tip peeking out at the top.

"Stay in town, Mr. Barlowe," the detective stated from behind them as someone opened the door to let them pass. "And be available for further questioning."

Silas didn't bother replying, his snort and *good luck* only inside his head. He'd taken out the trash, and it was time to deal with the adrenaline still coursing through his bloodstream that desperately needed an outlet.

2

Troy

A smart man, Mr. Barlowe didn't speak a word as they exited the police station. The spring air cooled Troy's heated face, and he glanced at his client, noting the workout clothing that he hadn't expected to see.

Noah's client came from money, Troy had read in his file before heading to the station. He also had plenty of his own and was known around town as a ruthless businessman—and playboy.

Troy had expected a suit and tie, considering it was a workday, or nice casual jeans and button-down at the least. But no. Silas Barlowe paraded around in a form-fitting T-shirt that outlined bulging shoulders and prominent pecs. And his mesh gym shorts left nothing to the imagination.

Queer as a four-dollar bill, Troy couldn't help his

body's reaction to all of Silas's splendid…lusciousness. Dark hair and arresting hazel eyes, one showing the beginnings of a black bruise. Broad shoulders, big enough to pin him down and take whatever he wanted.

Not my type, Troy lied to himself, hating the memory of how his dick had sprung to life from a mere handshake. The man had noticed his reaction too, much to Troy's annoyance.

Troy swallowed thickly against the desire rippling down his spine while fully stepping out into the Boston spring day.

Not having heard the story of why Mr. Barlowe had been detained for questioning, why he wasn't dressed in the threads the media always showed him in, Troy didn't know what to think.

But his body *still* did, and in front of the station was no place for a conversation about business—or otherwise.

"I'm assuming you caught a ride in a cruiser?" Troy asked, stopping on the sidewalk.

"Yep." Silas hunched against the cool breeze, the skin of his muscular forearms pebbling beneath Troy's gaze.

Troy ripped his focus off Silas's hairy arms—strong enough to break a man—and pulled his keys from his suit coat pocket. "I can take you wherever you need to go." He managed to keep his tone level rather than squeaking at the idea of being wrapped up against Silas's chest, those wide hands of his grasping his ass.

"Appreciate it." Silas followed along behind Troy, but awareness of the larger man's presence heated Troy's backside, causing his skin to cover in goosebumps.

No gaydar had pinged while Troy had quickly taken in Mr. Barlowe upon arriving at the interrogation room, but the man hadn't bothered hiding the interest in his eyes—or the slow smirk that suggested he wouldn't mind a little taste.

While the thought of being spread out for Silas Barlowe's pleasure pushed every single one of his buttons—

No, Troy lied.

Troy held himself to a high standard. No messing with clients. And he sure as hell wouldn't mess around with a known player who had the type of body he'd never be able to escape.

A shiver slid down Troy's spine, tempting him to relax just a little, but he lifted his chin, his footsteps steady as always even though his legs trembled.

It wasn't until the two sat enclosed in his cluttered BMW that Troy's outward confidence wavered.

Best to keep focused on the task at hand although the heat of the sexy man's stare sent all Troy's blood rushing south. His dick stiffened enough he shifted to adjust himself before starting up his car.

Troy Emerson didn't flirt with men like Silas after learning the possible outcomes the hard way back in high school. And although Silas turned his body on like the flip of a switch, Troy refused to be anything but professional.

"Would you like to fill me in, Mr. Barlow," he asked, "or do you prefer to wait to make an appointment with Noah? You're under no obligation to speak with me, but anything you state in this car is also covered by our confidentiality policy seeing as how I'm sure I'll be helping if needed."

"Silas, please."

Troy nodded without looking at his passenger and pulled out of his parking spot, fighting to steady his pulse when everything about Silas made him want to climb the man like a damn tree.

"And I'll gladly give you whatever you want." His tone, his insinuation, clenched Troy's asshole and left him lightheaded.

"Just honesty," Troy rasped, hating he revealed how Mr. Barlowe affected him.

His passenger let out a quiet chuckle, and Troy silently cursed himself while turning right onto Congress Street.

Mr. Barlowe stated the facts, offering Troy a quick run-down of the break-in, fight, and subsequent death of the intruder. While the story sounded cut and dry as self-defense, Troy knew there were three sides to every story. The two involved—and the truth.

Fortunately for Silas, the deceased wasn't able to tell his point of view.

"As long as they don't find any evidence to suggest otherwise—"

"They won't," Silas interrupted, his tone firm, cocky almost.

Troy glanced over him, taking a quick study of his strong profile, the thin blade of a nose, and the five-o'clock shadow that would feel luscious scraping across his skin. A shudder rippled through him, and Troy turned his attention back on the road.

"You seem quite sure of yourself," Troy stated quietly.

"Easily done when you've got nothing to hide."

Another glance didn't reveal anything more than certainty on Silas's face. Assuming he hadn't lied, there wasn't a thing to fear. Lucky for him, Massachusetts held self-defense laws that other states did not.

"So, who was the intruder?" Troy asked, hanging a left at the next intersection.

"No fucking clue."

"Any idea why he'd target your sister?"

"Could have been random," Silas suggested, his tone bored.

Too controlled for a man who'd just stabbed another to death.

"Guys are always after my sister's ass—she's gorgeous—and that gun suggested he didn't plan on leaving without getting whatever he wanted from her."

"You appear unaffected," Troy observed, hoping to slide beneath Silas's skin and encourage a reaction. "Odd, considering you took a man's life this morning."

"Fucker deserved it." A hint of spite inflected Silas's tone, raising the hackles on Troy's neck.

"You love your sister."

"She's all I have."

Troy hung a right onto Commonwealth Ave while considering Silas's claim. "You own a multibillion-dollar company. A penthouse in Boston, a house on Lake Winnipesaukee. One in Telluride and one in Tuscany."

"Did you take a few minutes to Google me before coming to the station, Troy?"

"I scanned your file."

"And what else did you learn?"

"Only facts, but I know who you are," Troy stated, having already put Silas Barlowe into a tidy box inside his head as he did with all men.

"And what am I?"

Someone who would do whatever necessary to bed Troy then discard him.

Troy slowed as he approached the address Silas had provided. "An overindulgent playboy who thinks he can get anything and any woman he wants."

"You don't mince words." A hint of admiration laced Silas's statement.

"Honesty is the best policy."

The heat of Silas's stare warmed Troy's face. "Always?"

He pulled up alongside Silas's Mercedes parked on the street in front of his sister's place and hit the four-ways. "*Always*," Troy replied firmly.

Even when your words weren't believed.

Yellow caution tape blocked off Grace's property, one cruiser, another unmarked car, and the forensics van still onsite.

The sexy as hell man shifted, angling toward him, and Troy steeled himself before giving Silas his attention.

"How's this for honesty, assistant attorney Troy Emerson?" Silas leaned forward, his lowered tone and the lust in his hazel eyes causing Troy's dick to swell back to full thickness again. "I thought I was straight as fuck and had never met a man I wanted to strip down to nothing but neediness until you walked through that door. Your pristine suit rumpled on the floor, every inch of your pale, pretty skin marked by my mouth and fingertips, and your hair mussed from being thoroughly *fucked*."

Troy barely managed to keep his shiver internal, and he forced a frown to furrow his brow. "I have zero interest in sating curiosity, and quite frankly, your confidence is off-putting, Mr. Barlowe."

"The pink on your cheeks says otherwise, *Mr. Emerson*."

Troy needed to swallow—hard—but refrained. "I will not fraternize with a client."

Silas flashed a grin at the breathless tone Troy hadn't been able to help, and hell if the man's smile wasn't the sexiest thing he'd ever seen. "Care to make a wager?"

Straightening in the driver's seat, Troy lifted his chin and glanced down over the muscles bulging beneath Silas's T-shirt. Luscious, tempting man—but off-limits. "Unlike you, I don't gamble unless it's a sure thing."

"But you *are* a sure thing," Silas assured him, his eyes hooded as he reached for the door handle. "You just don't know it yet."

His wink caused Troy's belly to flutter, keeping anger over Silas's assumptions from rising.

Silas Barlowe might not need apps to find a hook-up every night of the week with his money and his looks, but Troy wouldn't be swayed by Silas's smooth words or wicked hot body.

No matter how much his dick disagreed with his mind.

He'd given in to a similar man once before who ended up damn near ruining his life.

3

Silas

"Silas! What the hell happened?" Grace sounded ready to lose her shit over the phone.

Cell to his ear, Silas got a tumbler from his kitchen cabinet and hit the ice button on his fridge to fill it. "Where are you?" he asked, needing to check in with her before spilling the details about the attack.

"I'm at my friends—the police told me I couldn't go home, that there was a break-in, that you killed him—what the fuck!"

"Calm down, Grace. I'm okay. Everything is going to be fine." Silas poured Grey Goose into his waiting glass. "Get yourself a drink, and I'll fill you in."

His penthouse offered comfort, the best worldly

possessions money could buy, and Silas stretched out on his couch, glancing over Boston's skyline outside his living room's massive picture windows.

Once Grace assured Silas she was seated with a glass of red wine, he proceeded to tell her the exact same story he'd given the police from beginning to end. He ignored the twisting in his guts, knowing the vodka would soon ease it.

Grace sat silent for a few seconds after he finished. "Why did he break into my house? What was the guy after?"

"As far as we know, it was a random. He just got unlucky that someone bigger and stronger happened to be home."

"What's going to happen now?" she asked.

"The police will investigate, find jack shit to refute my claims, and that'll be the end of it."

"They won't press charges? Manslaughter or something?"

"It was self-defense," Silas assured her while studying the half-empty tumbler in his hand. The buzz needed to kick in and soothe the unease in his guts. "Even if they wanted to arrest me for murder, they wouldn't find the evidence to get that warrant."

"I can't believe this..." Grace let out a heavy sigh that sounded much more settled to Silas's ear.

"Everything will be okay," Silas repeated. "Don't worry about it. Just stay at your friend's house until the police say you can go back home. The police won't leave a trace of the attack—not a speck. Promise. You won't even know shit went down. I'll be sure to swing by next week and finish fixing that drain since I was so rudely interrupted."

Grace let out a soft laugh. "You're the best. Are you sure you're alright? He didn't hurt you or anything?

Silas sipped his vodka, ready to change the subject. "My ribs are a little sore, and I'll have a black eye to match yours, but that's it. How is it healing up by the way?"

"The bruising is pretty well faded."

"Did you enroll that damn dog in obedience school yet? Because if he headbutts you again, I might have to have a stern talking to with him."

More laughter filled Silas's ear, and he found himself smiling as warmth and tenderness welled inside him. Family was everything to Silas—he would have his little sister's back until she rested six feet under.

"Love you, Grace," he told her a few minutes later before hanging up.

"Love you too, Si."

Silas's smile faded as he lowered the cell and finished off his drink in one swallow. He got up from his couch for a refill before settling in to do what he'd planned on.

Learning all about Troy Emerson.

He wasn't on social media, Silas noted after a solid half-hour of searching. He should have been relaxed after his first vodka on the rocks and a hot shower, but his insides felt…antsy. Unnerved in a way he'd never experienced before.

It'd been one hell of a long day, fucked up in more ways than one. Stabbing someone to death. Falling into lust with a guy.

Pretty and sweet. Willowy and graceful.

Silas's dick swelled again at the memory of strawberry blond hair and those lips he wanted to slide his hard length between. He bet Troy would look hot as fuck on his knees, wide blue eyes peering up at him, tongue sticking out as if to beg for his cum.

An image flashed in his head of *him* dropping to his knees to taste the kid.

"Fuck." Silas slammed back the rest of his drink and gave into the need to jerk off to thoughts of a guy for the first time in his life.

Troy had captivated him, stolen his focus in a way no woman had ever done. Like a bizarre curiosity had zapped his dick with a surge of adrenaline, and Silas was powerless to fight the desire even if he'd tried to.

When Silas saw something he wanted, he didn't overanalyze. He took.

The image of swallowing down Troy's length

stayed rooted in his head, and every harsh stroke of his fist over his dick edged him in seconds.

Silas's balls seized, he swore again, and cum erupted up through his length, painting his T-shirt with stripes of milky white.

Head tipped back and gasping for air, he considered what he'd fantasized about the kid.

Not really a kid—he worked as an assistant lawyer for fuck's sake. One damn fine…what was his type called? Twinks?

Damn fine whatever society might label him, Silas thought.

He didn't feel a twinge of anything but acceptance over what he'd done. Female, male…he realized he didn't give a shit which way he swayed.

Or why it took an elfin angel to make him cross a line he'd never considered before.

He didn't know a thing about Troy—and he hated not having insight in a person who interested him.

"Hey, Siri, call Chávez," he stated in the quietness around him.

"Calling Chávez," his cell phone replied from the cushion beside him.

Silas picked up the phone with his clean hand, wiping cum off his other onto his silk lounge pants while ringing sounded in his ear.

"What's up, Silas?" his friend responded, the

private investigator he used on professional and personal levels alike.

"I got a name for you."

"Business or pleasure?"

Silas huffed a snort. "Pleasure—Troy Emerson. He works for Noah."

"Troy—as in a dude?"

"Yep."

"Pleasure, you said?" Chávez asked, his tone disbelieving.

"Yep."

His friend chuckled. "Coming to the dark side, Silas?"

"Hopefully coming in his ass before the weekend's over."

A burst of laughter hit his ear. "Maybe moving on from pussy will find you your soulmate. God knows you could use some *feelings*."

"Don't need shit other than a good fuck now and then," Silas shot back what he always said whenever his friend gave him a hard time. He loved the single life and had no interest in allowing anyone inside his head and heart. He would never admit to how Troy spun his head.

"Shame." Chávez let out an exaggerated sigh.

"I don't want to hear about your and John's date night," Silas grumbled. "Just find out the goods on Troy so I know how to lure him into my bed."

"You don't usually have issues with getting

someone to invite you into their bed. What's the problem with this one?"

"Troy is…the non-devious sort. Honest."

"Opposites *do* attract."

"Fuck off, Chávez."

A few more details, a lot of ribbing exchanged, and Silas hung up, trusting his friend to get him what he needed.

Instead of being worried over the investigation or the fact he'd stabbed a man in the throat, Silas showered for a second time. Jerked off again to thoughts of Troy grabbing his own ankles and begging for Silas's dick.

And he fell into slumber like a baby, his confidence assuring him he didn't have a thing to fear.

Chávez called the next afternoon, but Silas sat in a business meeting and couldn't answer.

He couldn't focus on the numbers his assistant went over, the proof of a new possible acquisition that he'd been looking forward to hearing about for over two weeks.

The cell dinged a few minutes after it quit ringing, and Silas wondered over the long as fuck message Chávez had left.

His investigator friend had found something, otherwise he'd have been short and to the point.

Silas couldn't sit still, unable to give his attention to the business at hand. "I'm sorry…can we finish this tomorrow?"

"Sure thing." His assistant gathered up the papers and files off of the conference table and walked out.

Silas picked up his cell and swiped it open. Sure enough, Chávez had left a message.

"So your boy toy—I mean boy, Troy—is twenty-six, moved back into his parent's house after graduating from law school, and now shares a place with a couple of roommates down near Allston. He's squeaky clean, except for one event in high school that probably explains his non-deviousness and honesty."

Silas thinned his lips, his brow furrowing.

"But I'll get to that in a second." Chávez went on to share a bunch of family shit and accolades, none of which Silas cared about. He couldn't give two shits if the kid graduated third in his class or that he'd come from blue-collar working parents who also hadn't done anything outside the law.

"So, back to that event," Chávez said, gaining Silas's full attention. "Troy was involved in a scandal with one of his teachers. Sexting, Face Timing, online sex sort of shit. But when the two truly crossed the line once Troy turned eighteen in his senior year, he claimed the guy forced him. One man's word against another, but the evidence of their past interactions got those charges dropped."

"Fuck." Silas scrubbed a hand down over his face, his gut instinct to feel sorry for the kid. He'd seen plenty of he said/she said scenarios in the workplace —but not one of the situations had been cut and dry.

"The teacher still lost his job, obviously, but he wasn't found guilty of sexual harassment and assault like Troy and his parent's lawyers had pushed for."

Silas muttered another curse, wondering how badly the whole affair had fucked Troy up, but Chávez wasn't done.

"The kid hangs out in that new gay bar—*Posh*— looking for hookups every Friday night like clock-work. And knowing you're hoping to enjoy his ass...*Posh* is on Beacon Street."

Shaking his head, Silas once more wondered how the fuck his friend found that kind of shit out in a matter of hours. *He* ought to be on the Boston PD. Too bad for them, Chávez preferred the gray shade when it came to black and white, same as Silas.

"If I had to make a guess," Chávez continued, "I'd say Troy has trust issues from that high school shit and is just as against finding a soulmate as you are. So, nutshell? If you get him in your bed, keep those *feelings* under lock and key like usual or you'll end up with a broken heart."

The message ended without another word, and Silas went into Venmo to send him his finder's fee even though Chávez hadn't asked him for it.

Posh. Friday night.

Silas glanced at his watch, deciding he could cut out of work early for a change.

He had a boy toy to claim for a night of debauchery.

Troy Emerson had more or less stated he didn't cross lines, but his body had obviously lusted to leap over one for Silas—and he wouldn't settle for anything less than hearing and seeing *that* bit of honesty spilling from Troy's lips.

Two hours later, Silas stepped into *Posh's* dim interior, freshly showered. He'd traded in his Armani suit for designer jeans and a nice light pink button-down since Silas expected Troy liked the color to have worn it himself the day before.

Leather loungers snuggled into groupings, a few high tables closer to the bar along the back wall, and the place was almost filled to capacity. Music played overhead that offered the smaller dance floor some action, but not so loud that guys couldn't mingle.

Silas had anticipated a meat market, more… sexual energy, but the patrons weren't blowing each other in dark corners or groping one another in the open. Even the couples grinding on the floor weren't doing so indecently. The atmosphere was indeed posh—and he liked the vibe more than he'd thought he would.

Once at the bar, Silas ordered a vodka on the rocks, and turned, taking in the dozens of guys through the dim lights and those flashing over bodies moving to the beat of sensual music. Only a few people sat by themselves.

Troy wasn't one of them.

Silas had expected as such. The kid was too damn pretty to miss out on a Friday night hook-up. He lounged at the other end of the bar with a ginger, a little too close, a little too intimate with one another. Face flushed, Troy angled toward him to converse, but their words got lost in the bar's din.

Silas sipped his drink, his stomach churning. Every muscle in his body tensed to head Troy's way, so he did.

Troy caught sight of him, his eyes widening with every stride Silas made to eat up the feet between them.

Ignoring the guy Troy had been talking to, Silas muscled between the two stools, his focus on those wide pale eyes that tightened his groin.

"Wh-what are you doing here?" Troy's breath smelled like strawberries and vodka, his voice nothing more than a slurred squeak.

Silas leaned in and kissed his forehead, filling his lungs full of…yes, strawberries and vanilla.

"What was *that* for?" Troy's voice cracked.

Goddamn, Troy was cute as fuck when flustered, half-drunk and sounding like a pubescent kid.

"Staking my claim," Silas replied with a wink, all up in Troy's personal space.

He frowned up at Silas but didn't back away.

"You don't have a claim," Troy hissed, but his swelled pupils stated he wished otherwise.

"Not yet." Silas turned to the man on his left, dissolving his smile and hardening his gaze. "You're in my seat."

The ginger got up without a word, taking his drink along with him, and didn't bother with a backward glance.

Silas settled onto the warm, vacated stool facing Troy, wanting to beat fists on his chest and declare victory. But he still had a major hill to climb before tumbling into bed with his prey.

"Quite rude," Troy muttered and finished off his martini, his Adam's apple bobbing. He flagged down the bartender while Silas studied him. His tongue wanted to taste the smooth, pale skin of his neck, and his teeth to sink into the throbbing pulse beneath.

Pink continued to stain Troy's cheeks, and his was hair styled perfectly, no tousled look like he'd already hooked up in the bar's bathroom. He wore a shirt and tie, and having learned about Troy's work ethic, Silas figured the kid had probably come straight from the office.

"Grey Goose martini?" The bartender asked before Troy could order, and he nodded his agreement.

Troy ignored Silas until he held his drink in his shaking hand when he finally glanced his way.

"Evan was a sure thing—thanks for ruining my night."

Once more, Silas leaned forward, his lips lifting in a smirk, lust simmering in his balls. "You don't have to go home alone tonight. *I'm* a sure thing."

4

Troy

Troy didn't doubt Silas's husky words that sent goosebumps racing over his skin. One plus he would give Silas—he was honest about how badly he wanted Troy and had been from the moment they'd met at the police station.

Cocky bastard pissed him off and made his body want to *get* off at the same time. He fucked with Troy's head more than anyone had before.

Less than a foot separated the two men, their knees pressed together, but Troy didn't pull away. Pleasantly buzzed, he didn't have the strength to put distance between himself and the driven Greek god whose hazel eyes hooded with a lust-filled look that promised a good time.

And fuck did Troy need it even if his sense of self-preservation screamed no.

He'd finished a long week at the office and an

even longer day buried under a shit ton of work. Noah knew how to take advantage of an associate who had big plans for their future, that was for damned sure.

Troy yearned for release with a bone-deep ache.

"Cat got your tongue, boy?" Silas asked, his smirk fixed in place while raising his tumbler for a swallow of whatever clear liquid he'd ordered over the rocks.

"I'm not a boy," Troy stated with a lift of his chin and sipped his drink, annoyed with how his voice had betrayed him when Silas had first shown up. He'd sounded unsure, off-kilter, exactly how his insides felt, stirred up by the confident man's presence.

"You look like you haven't had to shave a day in your life. Tell me"—Silas got all up in Troy's space again, causing his heart to race—"is the rest of your body as smooth as your gorgeous jawline?" He ran the back of his knuckles from Troy's chin to his ear, his touch a searing fire Troy couldn't escape.

Unable to help the shiver that rippled over him, Troy gulped. "Would your dick get hard if I said yes?" he heard himself ask, as breathless as a needy bottom—which he totally was when sucking down vodka, damn his libido. What had happened to his conscience? His desire to be the one in control?

Silas's left eyebrow cocked upward. "How many drinks have you had, Mr. Emerson? Because I gotta say…I rather enjoy this side of you." His hot breath caressed Troy's mouth.

"Two? Three?" Troy shrugged, his hand shaking slightly as he turned his attention forward to taste his martini.

"Are you drunk?"

"Not really."

Unfortunately. Troy had no idea how to handle Silas Barlowe—he was too much…too *everything*.

"Good." Silas grasped Troy's chin and turned his head. His gaze slipped to Troy's lips. "I believe you still owe me an answer to one of my questions," he murmured, the deep tone of his voice ticking off Troy's *yes, please* boxes.

Troy fought for calm, but…vodka. "About how I wax every bit of hair from my body?"

Damn him and his weakness on Friday nights.

"Fuck. You do, don't you?" A deep rumbled groan from Silas's lips caused wetness to leak from the tip of Troy's dick.

He let out a whimper without meaning to, cupping his bulge and squeezing. "Yes?" Troy squeaked.

Silas leaned in even closer, and Troy held his breath, his body sizzling like a live wire, every inch of his skin as tight as his grip on his dick.

"I'm already hard just from the sweet as honey scent of you in my nose and the taste of you still on my lips."

Silas's gentle kiss on Troy's forehead earlier contradicted the lust simmering in his eyes. A shiver slid down Troy's spine as he realized he could still *feel* the sexy man's mouth on him.

"You certainly don't hold back, do you, Mr. Barlowe?" Troy tried for normalcy in his voice and failed. At least he managed to tear his hand off his groin and fist it on the bar.

"Honesty is the best policy," Silas repeated Troy's words from the day before with a wink. "Which means I'm not done yet. To fully answer *your* question," Silas murmured, tugging on Troy's chin to part his lips, "the idea of your drawn-up balls and all that silky soft skin of your taint and ass ready for my tongue...fuck, yeah, it turns me on."

Troy fought to fill his lungs while curses rang between his ears. He needed to get the hell out of there, away from the worst temptation he'd ever faced in his life.

Silas Barlowe was ten times more aggressive than—

No. Not thinking about that, Troy told himself, instead focusing on the fact he'd become a man, one who knew his mind, one who wouldn't ever be manipulated again.

Nothing wrong with a little flirting...as long as he stayed in control.

"What else would you do with your tongue if you

get the chance?" he heard himself ask when he should have slipped away.

Damn vodka.

"Lick up the back of your dick," Silas murmured, his eyes darkening. "Probe your slit to see what you taste like."

"Fuck," Troy whispered, captivated by Silas's heady stare, his hand twitching to drop to his groin again.

"I'd do that too—you wouldn't even have to ask. Tongue, fingers, my dick, I'll give you whatever your pretty little ass desires."

"Silas…" Troy licked his lower lip, causing Silas's gaze to drop to his mouth once more.

"Yes?" Silas asked, rubbing his thumb over the wetness.

They both groaned.

Troy tugged away from his hold and downed the rest of his martini with a shaking hand, even though he already approached drunkenness. He flagged the bartender.

Alcohol was always the best excuse for stupid decisions, but Troy told himself it was for liquid courage to walk away.

As if.

Troy *needed* an excuse because there was no way in hell he could say no to smooth-talking Silas who dropped truth bombs without a care of who might overhear.

Wicked, wicked man had gotten under his skin, lessening the distaste Silas's type usually stirred up in his gut.

And he was probably deliciously endowed with a dick that would set his world straight…wait. Not straight…fill him up sounded *much* better.

Troy bit back a smirk. His body buzzed, his nerve endings zapping instead of numbing from the alcohol. One martini delivered—downed like water, and still, he couldn't ignore Silas and his body's natural reaction to being in too-close proximity.

A warm hand pressed against his back, and Silas scooted in, trapping Troy between his spread legs.

Too close…not near enough. Troy's eyelids fluttered shut with a sigh.

"I'm cutting you off, Troy."

"What? Why?" He slurred the words, blinking the bar back into focus.

Hot breath caressed Troy's ear, sending a shiver down his spine. "Because I won't have you so drunk you can't consent to my tasting every inch of your smooth skin."

"Oh, God." Troy let out a light giggle at his croaked words—he never giggled. He was an attorney for fuck's sake.

"Goddamnit, Troy." Silas stood and discretely adjusted his dick.

Yep. Endowed, just like Troy had assumed. He clenched his hole at the idea of sinking over Silas's length until their groins pressed together. "Yes, please," Troy whispered, gaze glued to the ridge straining along Silas's jeans.

Thick. Long.

His mouth watered.

A hundred-dollar bill slapped onto the bar beneath Silas's hand, and he grasped Troy's elbow.

Troy stood without being tugged, falling into the hardest chest…his hands found their way up Silas's torso as he leaned in closer, wanting to melt into all bulging muscle and bone.

Expensive cologne, the hint of soap on warm skin jolted need through Troy's balls. "Where are we going?" he slurred, not caring where Silas dropped his jeans and let Troy have his way with him—just as long as he did.

"I'm taking you home."

Home meant a bed. Classier than the bathroom stall hook-up he'd expected. "Mmm. Okay."

"Is your car here?" Silas asked.

Troy shifted through his buzzed—drunk—brain, trying to remember how he'd gotten to *Posh*. Perhaps he'd sucked down one martini too many. "Uber! I never drive on Friday nights. Duh." Another unintended giggle escaped him, damnit.

Silas wrapped an arm around Troy's shoulder and led him out into the cool night, but no amount of spring air laced with exhaust and the faint scent of saltwater could clear the fuzziness creeping into Troy's brain.

Stumbling steps, a firm grip on his hip as they walked down the sidewalk…

Parking lot. Mercedes, Troy realized. Silas's car.

The scent of leather and the spiciness of Silas's cologne wrapped around Troy, and smiling, he tipped his head back against the passenger seat.

An arm reached over him.

Seatbelt buckled.

"If you puke in my car, I'll redden your ass."

"I'm not into that shit." Troy murmured. That final martini had hit with a good right hook, he realized.

"Then I'll just have to hold you down."

"Mmm. *That* I could go for." Troy shifted on the seat, his ass already tingling. Wait—he didn't like getting spanked, and he sure as fuck wouldn't allow another man to restrain him.

Or would he? The thought of being at Silas's mercy might send Troy's sober mind straight to a no, but vodka-sloshed?

That was a whole other story.

"What's your address?"

Troy spilled it out, his mouth on autopilot, and seconds later, the vehicle moved beneath him. Still smiling, he enjoyed the darkness behind his eyelids, his imagination wanting to take a fantasy trip.

"I'd love to climb you like a tree," he murmured

the thoughts that moved through his head like a murky, slow-motion movie.

"Troy."

"Climb aboard and ride the hell outta you until you unload in my ass and I paint your abs with stripes of cum."

"Goddamnit, kid."

"Not a kid," Troy said with a singsong tone. He turned his head and opened his eyes, taking a few seconds to focus on Silas who stared straight ahead, his jaw clenched. "Are you going to take me to bed, Mr. Barlowe?"

"Yes."

"I *love* your honesty," Troy said, drawing out the L word with a wide grin, his body going all lax in the leather beneath him.

A muscle ticked in Silas's jaw. "I don't."

Troy's head attempted to split in half.

He cracked his eyelids apart and cursed the sunlight in his face. "The fuck?" Groaning, he rolled away from the window, not sure what day it was—or *where* he was.

Posh.

Silas Barlowe.

His eyelids shot open again.

Home, he realized as he focused on his bureau a few

feet away. Alone, he observed while blinking the rest of the room to life in his brain. Stripped to his underwear, he noted while running his hands down over his body.

Cottonmouth, a splitting headache, and no luscious ache in his backside.

Too much vodka.

And not enough dick.

His slacks, shirt, and tie from the day before lay neatly folded at the foot of his bed. A glass of water and the bottle of pain reliever he kept in his medicine cabinet waited for him on his bed stand.

"Goddamnit," Troy groaned, sinking back into his mattress again, an arm over his face. "I had you tucked into a nice, neat box, Silas. Why the hell did you have to force your way out?"

Was it possible Troy's gut had been wrong about him?

He hoped—and dreaded the possibility.

After downing the meds and the entire glass of water, Troy took a long, hot shower, checking himself for evidence of Silas loving on his body.

Nothing.

No bruising from fingers or mouths, no lingering redness on his ass from handprints—

"Fuck that shit," Troy muttered, even though his dick twitched at the image flickering in his brain of being at Silas's mercy.

Too much damn vodka had messed with his head

the night before, but thankfully Silas hadn't taken advantage of his weakness.

How could he have been so stupid?

Evan had been in the palm of his hand—a cute ginger, not aggressive or demanding…simply someone sweet looking to get off. They should have left earlier, before Troy had allowed himself that second martini.

But seeing Silas, how he'd stalked toward him, got all up in his personal space like he'd belonged there…Troy had been powerless against his wiles. Hate and lust had mingled in his brain over how easily Silas had sent Evan away and had assumed his place.

And all the things he'd said, the promises he'd made…

A shiver licked down Troy's spine, and he yanked aside the shower curtain a little harder than necessary.

No more mixing vodka and Silas.

Maybe he'd get lucky and never have to see the man again.

But he wanted to. Badly.

Troy shuffled into the small kitchen he shared with his two roommates. Both sat bleary-eyed and scruffy at their table, coffee mugs in hand. "Morning," he grunted.

They ignored him, without a doubt hungover as

well with how they partied every weekend, and Troy poured himself a cup.

"Were either of you around last night when my… friend brought me home?"

"Nope," they replied in unison.

That answered *that* question in Troy's brain. He must have been lucid enough to tell Silas where he lived, managed to pull the door keys from his pocket and point Silas toward which room was his.

The man had taken him to bed as promised—without taking *care* of him.

Troy couldn't decide which he found more disappointing. Silas escaping the box Troy had placed him in, or the fact he hadn't been sober enough to ride the man's dick until release.

No sense in crying over spilled coffee, his mom had always said with a smile. He looked forward to a family dinner with her and his dad later that night since he hadn't been home for going on three weeks.

Troy sipped his black brew and went back to his room, deciding he needed more beauty sleep before facing his mom. Otherwise, she'd be concerned he was coming down with something, same as she always worried whenever his usually perfect complexion betrayed his drinking.

With any luck, Silas Barlowe was indeed innocent in the self-defense affair from Thursday, he would meet with Noah alone the following week—

and Troy wouldn't even see him in passing ever again.

And Troy could hit *Posh* on a weeknight since he'd missed out on his weekly dick—same as he'd done for the previous two weekends due to exhaustion from the new job and his determination to make an impression.

But it was Silas, and that damn man alone, that haunted him as the days passed, keeping him from the nightlife after finishing up work late every day.

Troy decided missing out on the ride of his life was more disappointing than being wrong about how he'd judged Silas.

Maybe he'd get another chance to find out how Silas's tongue felt on his taint and ass…

A man could hope, even though his better sense said no.

5

Silas

Silas met with Noah Madden at his office early the following week. The information he'd shared with his young lawyer aligned with what he'd told the police and Grace.

Unfortunately, Troy wasn't around, so Silas didn't get to fill his eyes with the boy's beauty or sniff in the scent of strawberries that clung to him.

Silas had the chance to take what he wanted the Friday before, but of course his tiny shred of ethics kept his dick in his pants.

He'd tucked an unconscious Troy into bed, his ass safe from violation, his lips slacked and untasted.

But Silas didn't share any of that shit with Noah, because what did it matter? There was no active court case, no charges…Troy was not his attorney. There was no conflict of interest.

But he couldn't help remembering Troy asleep in

his bed, naked except for tiny pink briefs. Silas had stood and stared at for a long as fuck time. Every inch of Troy's slender form he'd uncovered, nipples that tightened in the cool air, hairless chest, and defined abs, had caused drool to flood his mouth. Silas had finally understood women's addiction to the V of muscle that led to his boxer briefs.

Troy's had called out to his tongue, and more than anything, he wanted to bury his face against the kid's groin, breathe him in—and enjoy a taste of dick, something he'd never considered before.

But Silas had denied himself.

The kid didn't reach out to him to thank him for getting him home safely—and not taking advantage of his stupor like a lot of other assholes would have done.

Troy's silence didn't turn Silas off, though. He looked forward to their next interaction.

The rest of the workweek passed faster than Silas expected—all remained quiet with the police investigation. He went forward with his newest acquisition, but the promise of taking over a business, rebuilding, then reaping the monetary reward didn't swell a sense of satisfaction inside him like usual.

When Friday rolled around again, he dressed for success, ready to fulfill his fantasies and find out what it was about Troy that turned his eyes away from the idea of a woman in his bed.

He wanted Troy beneath him.

Begging to be fucked.

Every night that week, he'd jerked off thinking about that elfin waif. Sinewy muscle, narrow waist, the enticing bulge beneath pink briefs...

Silas wondered what other color underthings Troy wore and cursed himself for not rifling through the kid's bureau to find out for himself. He'd stolen panties a time or two, but the idea of shooting spunk all over the material Troy hid beneath his pressed suits...

Fucking fine fantasies Silas wanted to come to life—and what Silas Barlowe wanted, he got one way or another. Even if it meant resorting to shades of gray.

Posh was hopping, same as it had been the week before, but Troy sat by himself in one of the black lounge chairs, a scowl on his face, the air around him stating "uninterested" loud and clear.

Another pink button-down tucked into jeans that Silas hoped to peel off him by night's end.

Silas got himself a drink and strolled over regardless of the *no-touchie* look on Troy's face. No widened eyes met his that time, but Troy sipped and stared him down over the rim of his martini glass while Silas approached.

"You're putting off major unapproachable vibes tonight, kid." Silas sat on the lounger beside him without asking if the seat was taken.

Troy's gaze flicked over Silas's body, no hint of

annoyance—or interest—in his eyes as he lowered his glass. "Shitty week."

"You and me both." Silas swirled the vodka in his tumbler, studying Troy's face. A bland expression remained, but color stained his high cheekbones, promising he wasn't completely unaffected by Silas's presence. "Work?"

"Busy as hell. Two big cases hanging over the firm's head. Noah told me you met with him on Monday afternoon, and you better hope nothing comes of that investigation into the man you killed. We're swamped as it is."

Silas hadn't been watching the news, and he hadn't gotten called in for further questioning. "There's nothing to worry about on that front," Silas assured him.

"I'm not worried for *you*," Troy snapped.

Someone needed to get laid, Silas thought, ready to offer, but Troy opened his mouth first.

"Sorry." The kid—not a kid—let out an exhale and studied his martini. "I'm sure you were just looking out for your sister—you really love her." Troy didn't ask a question, but Silas nodded.

"She's all I have." Silas decided to allow a bit of vulnerability in the hopes it would help break down the wall Troy had erected between them. Except for the Friday before, when he'd been drunk off his ass and Silas had ended up carrying him to his bedroom. "There's nothing I wouldn't do for those I love, and she's the only one I could rely on since childhood."

"What about your parents?"

You didn't get from some people without giving, Silas reminded himself. He usually avoided those types, but Troy intrigued him enough he allowed his barriers to lower a bit. "They were neglectful. Too busy with work and spending their money to pay attention to their kids."

Troy eyed him with more interest than Silas had expected. "Were...past tense?"

"They both died in a plane crash in Switzerland years ago."

"My condolences."

Silas shrugged off Troy's words and swallowed down some vodka. "It didn't change my and Grace's lives much. They were rarely around anyway."

"Still." Troy pursed his lips again, studying his drink.

Silas held his silence, allowing the kid to decide whatever it was he considered sharing in return.

"I was lucky in that regard," he finally said.

Thanks to Chávez, Silas had already learned that truth, but he wasn't about to let the young attorney know he'd had a private investigator look into his life. "You have a good relationship with your parents?"

"Yeah." Troy glanced around the bar. "Blue-collar type. Hardworking with high morals."

"They sound like decent people."

"The best," Troy said, returning his focus to Silas. "They supported me when I came out."

"With your love of the color pink, I'm sure they'd already guessed."

"They did." A soft smile tilted Troy's lips upward. "My parents assumed before I labeled myself. It's a shame more parents aren't the same."

"You're one of the lucky few."

Troy sipped his martini, seeming more at ease, the whole *untouchable* vibe fading a bit. "My best friend Chase struggled. He's a twink like me—we grew up in the same neighborhood." Eyeing the rim of his glass, Troy frowned. "His father bullied him his entire childhood, and it took years of therapy for him to get his head right."

"I'm sure it helped having you as a friend though."

"Yeah. Chase and I were pretty much inseparable back then. You should see him now." Troy's furrowed brow smoothed out, and a hint of happiness lit his eyes for the first time since Silas had sat down. "He started lifting weights, met this guy named Zeke, a Christian counselor who fell in love with another guy—angsty as fuck story—then got involved with Humanity House where Zeke works."

"That's the LGBTQ home in Malden, isn't it?" Silas asked, remembering Grace talking about its expansion the year before when two gay pop stars helped celebrate its opening.

"One and only." Troy's smile faded. "Chase moved to Philly a week ago and is studying for his behavioral science degree. He wants to be a counselor and help kids like Zeke has been doing."

"Why Philly?"

"The owner of Humanity House is from there and is organizing another home near where he grew up. Chase's asshole dad passed, so he got some money for college and was ready to start over somewhere new." Troy shrugged, but Silas read the hurt in his eyes.

The kid missed his friend.

Silas ignored the tug inside him to ease that look on Troy's face. He just wanted in the twink's bed—or him in Silas's bed. That's what he told himself, anyway. "So what do you do for fun besides hunt for hook-ups on Friday nights?"

"Trying to make me feel better by changing the subject?"

"I'm partial to your smile." Silas's focus slipped to Troy's mouth.

"Oh?"

"Yeah. You've got sexy lips—especially that upper one that looks like you got stung by a bee."

And was that a hint of...lip gloss? Silas stared, sexual tension returning in the silence between them like a gusting nor'easter. His dick took interest, all thoughts of vulnerability and barriers wiped from his brain.

Silas swallowed down the rest of his vodka but couldn't tear his attention off what he wanted on his tongue.

"It's strawberry flavor, in case you were wondering," Troy said with a smirk.

A jolt of lust jerked Silas's dick at the thought of licking every trace from his pretty mouth—or having that gloss smeared all over his length. "I don't suppose I could get a taste?" he asked, lifting his focus upward.

Troy stared at him, but no annoyance or disinterest closed his eyes off. "I'm not available to be the curiosity that sates your kitty side."

"Kitty side." Silas snorted. "I'm not curious—I know I want you, and I don't give two shits about what's in your pants. Actually, I take that back. I'm anxious as *fuck* to wrap my hands around your dick."

Troy shifted in his seat, gaze flicking to Silas's groin. "You want a taste of that too, huh?"

Silas adjusted his erection, grinning when Troy's lips parted on a quick inhale. "Fuck, yeah."

Troy huffed out that lungful of air just as fast. "Goddamnit, Silas, why do you have to be so sexy?" His pale eyes lifted to Silas's, the *need* rising even higher between them.

"It's in my genes."

A smirk flitted over Troy's mouth, but he squashed it. He couldn't hide the interest on his face though. "What else is in your jeans?" His breathy voice couldn't have been more of an aphrodisiac to Silas.

"A hard, leaking dick that wants to be buried so far up your ass you won't remember the difference between illicit and iniquitous."

Troy groaned. "That's it." He sat his half-full martini glass onto the small table beside him, shaking his head as though disappointed in himself—but mind made up, regardless. "Let's go."

Being vulnerable and opening up for the win, Silas thought with a grin. It hadn't even hurt, and if he was honest with himself, he'd kind of enjoyed their little personal chat that left him wanting more.

Silas followed, hot on Troy's heels out of *Posh* like he'd been at the police station the week before.

Adrenaline hummed through his bloodstream, tension stringing him tight. The idea of something new, of finally getting the kid where he wanted him, caused lust like he'd never known to rage through his body.

He hadn't lied about his hard, leaking dick. Wetness smeared inside his boxer briefs—and he couldn't wait for Troy to get a taste of him too.

6

Troy

Thick silence filled Silas's car interior. Troy sat in the passenger seat, hands on his thighs, his pulse thrumming as they drove toward Silas's condo where they'd agreed to go since Troy had roommates.

Even though they'd shared a bit of personal shit, Troy's head warred with his choice. He couldn't deny wanting what Silas promised or the magnetic pull between them, and Silas *had* escaped that box Troy had put him in.

Shit. Troy shifted on the leather beneath him. "I, um…never thanked you for last Friday night," he said, his voice barely more than a whisper.

"My pleasure."

Troy glanced over at Silas, his brow furrowed over yet another peek into Silas's character. "But it wasn't, was it?"

Silas met his gaze.

"Pleasure, I mean," Troy added. "Because you didn't take advantage of me."

"Who said I didn't?" Silas asked, turning his attention forward.

Troy opened his mouth—and snapped it shut again. His ass hadn't been violated, that he knew for fact…but strangely, he didn't believe Silas did more than undress him before putting him in his bed.

There'd been no evidence to prove otherwise.

"You enjoy conquering what you set out to do." Troy worked on his thoughts out loud. "Win every game in life."

"Yes," Silas agreed without hesitation.

"You're the type who watches his enemies' eyes— or prey's—when finally getting them where you want them."

A smirk twitched Silas's lips—and Troy expected he'd hit on a serious truth of his nature. "So I couldn't have possibly chosen to do the right thing with your drunk ass because I'm an honest man?"

Troy wouldn't have thought so after their first interaction, but having learned a little about Silas over the week—his supposedly anonymous donations to charities, all the good things Noah had said about his character when he'd asked—and the personal information Silas had shared over their drinks…

"I may have placed you in a box you don't belong

in," Troy admitted, knowing he tended to do too often with people. It was what kept him safe after being too trusting.

Silas shot him a quick, quizzical look. "Did you just admit you were wrong?"

"I said *may*," Troy corrected. "The truth of you still remains to be seen."

"But you *are* interested in seeing."

Troy bit his tongue but decided there was no point in holding back. He was going to get the curious kitty out of his system and move on, thank you *very* much. "Every inch of your god-like body."

Silas barked out a laugh which caused Troy to do the same. They shared another lingering look that heightened the sexual tension between them to the smoking point.

"You might want to focus on the road, Silas," Troy stated with a little sass atop his breathiness. "I would prefer to get to your condo in one piece. High hopes, and all."

"You won't be disappointed," Silas promised with a wink.

And, he was back to his cocky playboy attitude.

Troy didn't give two shits. He hadn't gotten laid in…three weeks? Four? His ass ached to be stuffed. Destroyed.

Silas hadn't been charged with anything, no case file laid on Troy or Noah's desk…so why not fulfill their mutual lust?

He would fill himself with Silas's dick, get off on it, then walk away. Consensual sex—and hopefully one hell of a release. With the bulge Silas packed, Troy didn't doubt he'd enjoy himself.

Yes, please, and thank you.

"Almost there," Silas murmured and grinned as though he could hear Troy's thoughts.

"You can take the long way around the block," Troy said with a feigned air of uncaring. "I'm in no hurry."

"What happened to that *honesty is the best policy?*" Silas asked, laughter in his voice.

Troy let out a humph and crossed his arms.

Ten minutes later, Silas unlocked his condo door and stepped back, allowing Troy to enter first.

The place screamed money, sprawled in an open-concept with fancy art work tactfully hung. An entire section of wall held windows overlooking Boston, the city lights illuminating the living room area directly ahead. A chef's kitchen sat on the left with high end appliances, and a bedroom through the open door on the right revealed a king-sized four-poster bed with folded silk sheets.

Troy took two steps that way—

Silas spun Troy and attacked his mouth, pressing his back against the front door.

Heat and sparks ignited in Troy's stomach, blood rushing straight to his dick at the taste of vodka and pure male virility on Silas's insistent, seducing tongue. He grabbed hold of Silas's hair and tugged, needing to be closer.

Silas had promised a mind-blowing dicking down, and Troy had zero intention of stepping outside Silas's condo until he got it. Their tongues dueled, hot breaths and heady moans buzzing the silence around them. Mind-blowing perfection, better than Troy had expected or hoped. If Silas could use his dick as well as he did his mouth, Troy was in for one hell of a night.

"Strawberries." Silas groaned against his lips. "You're fucking delicious, Mr. Emerson." He occupied Troy's lips to keep him from replying a ditto, his hands dropping to Troy's aching dick. Yes, please and thank you.

Silas had claimed to want a taste of that too.

Troy's hands shook as he unzipped his slacks, desperate to free himself—and Silas took over with steady movements, slowly jerking him in time with his probing tongue sliding along Troy's. Control—fuck, did Silas have it over himself *and* Troy.

But no prickles of alarm raised the hairs on Troy's neck, no sixth sense to escape a big bad wolf. Silas might *be* big, might appear bad, but he was luscious caramel wrapped up in dark chocolate. Decadent. Addictive.

Every sensual move Silas made caused whimpers to escape Troy. He wanted to climb the man. Impale himself on that dick—

Silas tore his lips off Troy and sank to his knees in a fluid motion like he'd been born for it. Slow enough to tease but without a hint of hesitancy.

"Oh, God." Troy panted, staring at the dark head in line with his aching groin.

"I've never had a cock in my mouth before," Silas said, his tone haggard while taking him in hand, his thumb rubbing along Troy's length, "but I haven't been able to think about anything else."

Wet heat closed over the tip of Troy's length. "Fuck." He stared in the dim light as Silas sucked him into the back of the throat. "Oh, fuck…fuck." He grabbed hold of Silas's hair, fighting the need to thrust like a horny teenager getting his first blowjob.

Silas gagged, and Troy's balls seized up. "Holy *fucking* shit, Silas."

"Mmm," Silas hummed at the pre-cum oozing from Troy's slit, hollowing his cheeks and sucking as he lifted. "Fucking delicious," he repeated on a moan and filled his mouth again.

Troy's head thumped against the door, and he held Silas's in his hands, needing something to ground him as he panted for breath, his mind shattered to fragments. For never having sucked a dick before, Silas rated a solid ten out of ten, working Troy's entire length until his knees shook and every other exhale included a whispered curse.

All tongue and suction, no grazing teeth or

fumbling…Silas was a god even though he worshiped Troy.

I'm done, Troy thought while fighting to restrain himself. Officially ruined by the man he hadn't thought he'd wanted.

Silas backed off with a pop and nuzzled lower, his nose running over Troy's balls. "Bare…just like you'd said."

Troy widened his stance, biting his lower lip to keep from begging to be owned. Claimed. Breeded. Fuck, he needed it like his body did oxygen.

Silas knew what he wanted anyway—sucked his finger and found Troy's puckered hole.

"Yes…oh yes, please," Troy groaned, unable to help himself, lost to the supposed playboy's generosity.

"I'm going to wreck this," Silas murmured and drew one of Troy's balls into his mouth while sliding his finger into Troy's ass.

"Oh, shit…shit…shit…" Troy gasped and cursed with every probe, the firm rubs over his prostate. "I'm going to come…fucking hell, Silas, so good. God, I need…"

"Give it to me." Silas closed his mouth over Troy's dick again and took him deep enough to gag.

Cum erupted from Troy. "Fuck! Silas…" He thrust, too far gone in his climax to consider Silas's cock-sucking virginity. Not a care over if Silas had ever tasted spunk before crossed Troy's mind as shot after shot of ejaculate flooded Silas's mouth.

Fire raced across his skin, every contraction in his balls pulling grunts from his parted lips.

"Goddamn," he rasped out, finally opening his eyes as one last spurt left him and Silas pulled his finger from his ass.

Empty. Spent. Fucking perfect.

Silas stared up at him, his eyes pupil-blown, his mouth still full of dick. He lathed and suckled, keeping them connected—physically and somehow spiritually—until Troy had to tap out against Silas's head from sensitivity. One last suck extended Troy's softening length away from his body.

"Fuck, Silas." Troy whimpered, and Silas released him, pushing once more to his feet.

Endorphins and adrenaline coursed through Troy, robbing him of everything but the thought of *more*. So much more.

Grabbing hold of Silas's hair, Troy yanked him close, shoving his tongue into his mouth to taste his spunk on Silas's tongue. Hands found his ass and yanked him up—and Troy willingly wrapped his legs around Silas's waist as they continued to eat at one another like men starved of sustenance.

Troy might have had one of the best climaxes known to man, but his hole ached to be filled. He wanted to forget legal terms, his damn name, everything but the energy flaming between them.

"Silas, take me to your bed—"

Someone pounded on the door at Troy's back, and the two men stilled, blinking at one another, their breaths loud in the sudden silence

"Boston PD!" a voice hollered, causing Troy to flinch.

"Fuck." Silas's hold eased on Troy's ass.

Troy found his feet and scrambled to shove his spent dick back inside his slacks while stepping away from the entryway.

"Troy?" Silas's voice strained.

Brain still hazed, Troy fought to focus, to still his racing heart and the tremors from adrenaline flooding his system.

The pounding sounded again.

"Open the door, Silas," Troy said, his voice shaky as hell.

A flash of…fear, perhaps, flitted over Silas's eyes before blinking out. He turned away from Troy, his chest rising on a slow inhale, and did as told.

Detective Marsh from Boston's police department pushed into the condo first, a wicked gleam in his eyes and a grim grin on his face as a few other cops filed in behind him. "Silas Jonathan Barlowe, you're under arrest for the murder of Brian Parsons."

Time seemed to slow, and Troy's breaths sounded loud in his ears, fuzzy as though beneath water. Like in the movies, movement went liquid.

Silas allowed himself to be manhandled—spun

around like a swirling eddy, cuffs locking over his wrists, the clink reaching Troy's brain.

Muffled murmurs…Miranda rights, Troy realized, the detective's voice slowly coming to volume and clarity.

Troy's brain fired back to life, but he ignored Detective Marsh explaining the search warrant that allowed the other cops behind Troy to rifle through Silas's personal belongings.

One knock had interrupted lust and greed, demolished heightened senses ready to indulge. Responsibility, reality, crashed into Troy, but rather than be swept away in the tide, he found his footing. Reminded himself of who—what—he was.

Silas's shoulders and spine might still be straight, unbowed beneath arrest as he stood with his back toward Troy, but he needed him, needed his calm, his support.

Detective Marsh finished his little speech.

"Don't say a word, Silas," Troy stated firmly, but his hand shook as he held it outstretched for the warrant.

"Mr. Barlowe?" the detective asked Silas who jerked his head in a nod, giving him permission to hand it over.

The detective slapped the papers against Troy's palm. He quickly scanned the documents as officers continued to work in the condo behind him, opening drawers and rifling through Silas's things.

Silas Barlowe, playboy bachelor, and protector of his sister had landed his ass in deep shit.

Lips pressed tight to keep a disappointed exhale trapped, Troy lifted his head. Silas had turned, and his gaze snagged on shuttered hazel eyes. Troy found his heart believing Silas in the short time they'd connected.

Hopefully, he hadn't allowed his better judgement to be blinded by lust.

Troy held Silas's stare, desperate for the man to see his desire to support him on his face. Time once more seemed to drag to a crawl, but it couldn't pass slow enough as the energy from earlier radiated between the distance separating them.

A million promises flooded Troy's mind, words he wanted to spew to edify and encourage Silas, but he held himself in check regardless of the need that flared in Silas's steady gaze. Beyond lust, beyond the want for release…desperation of a different sort.

And Troy ached to give him everything.

"I'll call Noah," Troy whispered the one thing he could in that moment, his throat tight.

And prove to you that you can rely on me too.

Without another word spoken between the three of them, Detective Marsh led Silas out of the condo, and Troy's shoulders sank with a heavy exhale.

He allowed himself a brief moment to wallow in the tumble from the mountain top with Silas to the deep valley below. But Troy had learned how to pull himself out of darkness, to chase the light even when it seemed there wasn't one ahead of him.

Troy straightened his shoulders and held his spine as rigid as Silas's had been. He hadn't spoken the vows echoing in his head as they'd stared at each other, but he had every intention of observing every damn one.

It was time to get to work and keep the man he hadn't gotten nearly enough of out of the trouble he'd landed himself in.

7

Silas

Silas didn't sleep worth a shit. The taste of the elfin waif lingered on his tongue long after the jail shut down, leaving quieter echoes of shuffling and snoring rather than voices around him.

Charged for murder.

How? What possible evidence could that detective asshole have found? There wasn't any. Couldn't be.

And yet he lay on a narrow cot in a goddamn jumpsuit rather than sprawled on his bed beside a sated boy he couldn't get off his mind. Rather than stressing over the situation he found himself in, Silas chose to focus on earlier in the evening prior to his arrest.

The opening up and sharing with Troy while having drinks at *Posh*.

Their light banter that had come easily and proved enjoyable.

The softest, hungriest lips Silas had ever tasted.

He wanted more. Ached for it even while lying in jail surrounded by cold cement and air scented with sweat and fear.

A heavy exhale relaxed Silas's muscles, and he closed his eyes to memories of rumpled strawberry blond hair and hazed blue eyes peering down at him while he'd swallowed down his first cock.

The need to come had tightened his balls, but the night turned into morning without his seeking release. But as the hours passed, his thoughts of drugging kisses and sex faded into the new reality ahead of him.

He doubted a conviction, but what if a jury found him guilty?

What if he faced years behind bars and he was unable to pursue his newfound addiction?

What would happen to Grace if he didn't have his freedom to protect her?

Nausea roiled through his guts, keeping him from sleep. For the first time in his life, Silas's usual confidence fractured, and by Sunday night, Silas had reached his limit of self-control and fought to keep his placid, assured façade in place.

He needed a stiff drink. To get laid. To check in with his baby sister.

If convicted of murder, being in constant want with no chance of fulfillment would be his new norm—an unacceptable one. A fucking horrible future lacking in all of Silas's favorite things.

Sleep didn't come that night, and Monday morning found him before a judge for his bail hearing. He held his shoulders back and chin lifted—but his insides twisted tight and bowels gurgled.

Noah Madden showed up in a pristine suit rather than the angelic boy Silas had hoped to see, furthering his inner cramping.

A bond was set, and two hundred and fifty thousand got Silas's ass from behind bars.

For the time being.

Bright sunlight hit his face when he stepped outside, the taste of freedom racing through his system and once more giving him hope. He blinked —and found Troy waiting beside Noah's car. Relief flooded through him, easing some of the tension in his neck and shoulders.

Troy's eyes were wide and filled with concern and a shit ton of heat while he glanced down over Silas.

Goosebumps rose over Silas's body even though the sun warmed his skin. His cock hardened for the first time since Saturday morning.

Noah cursed and pointed at the vehicle as though he could feel the sexual energy and longing between

Troy and Silas. "Get in the car, both of you. Don't look, don't blink, don't talk, get in the car."

Troy opened the back door, and Silas filled his lungs with the scent of strawberries and vanilla while moving past him to slide across the seat. Troy settled his fine, tight ass beside Silas, enclosing them in silence. Their gazes locked, sending goddamn butterflies of all things through Silas's stomach.

Noah cursed again from the driver's seat and mentioned something about heading to his office and not speaking until they arrived.

Mutual desire and more that Silas couldn't put a name to filled the air between him and Troy. A connection he'd never experienced before. Almost… tangible and thicker than the insta-lust he'd felt the first time he'd laid eyes on the kid.

Yet another curse rang out, a hand hitting the steering wheel.

A grin snuck onto Silas's face while Troy winced. His boss was pissed at the obvious sexual tension between them, but Silas thrived on it.

Wanted more of it.

They arrived at the high-rise on Federal Street that housed Noah's office, and Silas still hadn't put a name to the feelings coursing through him.

Troy turned away first, breaking eye contact in order to open the door.

The scent of exhaust, grease, and cigarettes wiped the sweetness of Troy's skin from Silas's nose as he climbed out behind the younger man into the parking garage.

Noah's glare flitted between Silas and Troy as they moved to exit the building, and Silas opened his mouth to defend what he and Troy had going on. An upheld hand from Noah cut Silas off from speaking.

"Not. A. Word," Noah demanded. "When we are in my office and I have control over who overhears, we will talk."

No man but Silas's lawyer would ever control him so easily.

Fifteen floors slid beneath them as the elevator took the three men to the office of Madden Law. A minute later, Noah closed and locked the three of them up in privacy.

"Okay, first I want to point out I don't know and mostly I don't care what is going on, except where it affects your case," he growled out, pointing at the two chairs across from his desk.

Silas and Troy both sat.

"Do you mean the entirety of my case, Noah? Or didn't you have time to investigate any of it?" Silas asked, not bothering to hold back the sarcasm from his words as he settled his ass into the chair Noah had indicated. The twisting in his guts started up again as he glared at his attorney.

"Oh, don't worry Silas, I've kept up with your case." Noah crossed his arms and leaned against his desk, his stare hard. "I've kept up with the potential charges. What I don't understand is why Troy was in your condo when you got arrested in the evening? Or why he looked ready to combust when he saw you come out today?"

Troy's gasp had Silas wanting to grab his hand and squeeze, but Silas dug his fingers into his thighs. "You can be upset with me, Noah. I get that I've made things complicated, but Troy has done nothing but try to do the best by your firm." He bit the words out.

"Troy will not be working on your case from now on," Noah stated what Silas had expected. "He can't. We will get eaten alive by the district attorney. This stops you from having to answer to any specifics…"

Silas glanced over at Troy whose face had paled, leeching away the delicious flush from his high cheekbones.

The desire to bring color back to Troy's face hit Silas hard.

He nodded, ready to get the fuck out of there. "Fair enough, what else do you need from me Noah?"

"I'm going to need to talk to your sister."

Silas jerked his focus back toward Noah, his insides going cold.

"She hasn't had contact from police to give a statement. She hasn't been contacted by us either, and that's not good. I'm going to need access to her and the security cameras."

"Done, but she doesn't testify," Silas stated firmly. "She doesn't need to be dragged through the circus with me."

"I will do my best to keep her from being called, but that still requires me to talk with her. You killed someone in her townhouse, Silas. I will need some information to firm this up. I'm very confident in this case, but not without knowing all the information." Noah glared at Silas.

"Fine. I'll tell Grace to expect your call, but you need to soften your approach when you talk to her. If you upset her, I will fire you."

"In case you haven't noticed," Noah said, moving to stand directly in front of Silas, "my intentions, and in fact, my very occupation, is based on making sure you don't do time. If you think I'd somehow come at your sister negatively, you're not understanding how this is different from your business dealings. If you wish to hire different representation, you can."

"I don't, but my sister isn't me. She's not used to any of this." And Silas would do everything within his power to protect her from harm—physically or emotionally. "She's a veterinarian, and her entire life she's been dedicated to helping animals, not navigating shit-bags and legal systems. She doesn't deserve any fallout for something I caused."

"Fair enough, and I will be as gentle as I can be," Noah promised before ordering him and Troy from his office, muttering something about needing caffeine. He hadn't even finished speaking before Troy escaped, Silas hot on his heels.

No words passed between the two men, and Silas followed the younger attorney back to the parking garage as though of the same mind. Troy's tense shoulders appeared how Silas's felt, hitched up with anxiousness, the kind brought on by need for sexual gratification.

Silas had gone too fucking long since emptying his balls, and there was only one place he planned on releasing.

Troy unlocked his car. "Sorry about the mess…" He grabbed an empty takeout bag and coffee cup from the passenger seat, tossing them into the back.

Silas climbed in and adjusted his aching dick with a grimace before buckling up. "My place," he commanded, his tone not allowing for argument.

"Integrity demands I avoid you until this is all over, but I don't want to." Troy's voice was no more than a whisper.

Silas studied his profile as Troy pulled out into traffic, wondering which *honesty* Troy would lean toward if pushed—ethics concerning work or his lust for Silas. "Why?" he asked, needing to know but for his mind, not to stroke his ego.

Troy swallowed audibly. "Something about you makes me…feel rebellious."

A smirk spread on Silas's lips, a sense of confidence flooding through him. Troy wanted Silas beyond his moral soundness, and Silas teetered on the edge of choice.

Push Troy into gray areas or allow him to set himself on the same path he'd taken throughout his life?

"Are you okay?" Troy asked, glancing at Silas quickly before returning his focus to the road. "The weekend behind bars wasn't too awful?"

Concern showed in Troy's voice and eyes, enough that Silas knew he would end up in Silas's bed regardless of his desire to do what was right in the eyes of man. But a little enticement couldn't hurt.

Besides, the elfin angel's reactions always stirred Silas's blood.

"I need to shower and sleep, but I can put off the latter if it means I get another taste of your cum."

Troy let out a whimper and pressed down on his groin. "I have to go back to the office."

"Come to me later?" Silas asked rather than demanded. He knew he wasn't alone in his feelings and wanted Troy to come to him of his own volition.

It took a full five minutes for Troy to respond, but Silas practiced patience that he rarely did in order to give Troy that time to deliberate.

"I-I can't, Silas."

He could, Silas told himself along with a silent curse.

He would.

No more words passed between them, and Silas texted his sister while his building's elevator took him to the penthouse suite on the top floor. Since Grace lived under a rock except for her work, she must not have caught the news over the weekend— or the released name of the man he'd killed.

She would have called him otherwise.

The thought started up those damn cramps in his guts again, but he swallowed down the rising anxiety in order to keep his fingers from shaking while texting her.

He let her know his lawyer would be contacting her but didn't go into details or mention his three nights behind bars. That would only flip her out, same as it had done to his usual confidence, and he knew Mondays at the clinic kept her on her toes.

Silas stripped off his clothes from the Friday before and stepped beneath the hot spray of his shower, closing his eyes as water beat on his body from six different heads. Tension from the situation slowly drained from his shoulders, but the relentless throb in in his balls demanded attention.

A bit of conditioner slickened his pulls on his aching length, and he leaned against the cool tile with a forearm while thinking about Troy on his knees, plump lips parted, pink tongue sticking out for a mouthful.

Silas gave the imaginary boy what he wanted, groaning his name and shuddering with every spurt of cum ripping up through his dick.

Next time he came, he vowed to himself, it would be inside Troy's tight, hot ass.

8

Troy

A war battled in Troy's mind.

He needed to be involved in his case to show Silas that he could depend on him. To prove someone other than Grace had Silas's back, because Troy desired the man to the point his bones literally ached.

But taking an active part in defending him against the District Attorney's office meant no fraternizing, even though Noah hadn't outright demanded he stay away from Silas. If they attempted an affair in secret and got found out, his reputation as well as Silas's would be ruined.

"Fuck." Troy drove into his spot at the parking garage and scrubbed a hand down over his face. "Fucking fuck."

He heaved a heavy exhale and shoved his door open, determined to get direction from his boss.

He found Noah still in his office but readying to leave, probably to meet with Silas's sister.

"I need to be involved in this case, Noah."

His boss glanced his way, his face stern. "You can't if you're fucking Silas."

A shot of lust hit Troy's groin, and he swallowed back a growl of annoyance. "I have to do *something*," he stated through gritted teeth, even while nerves had his insides trembling.

Noah retrieved his keys from the desk where he'd thrown them earlier. He turned, studying Troy.

Chin lifting, Troy met his stare, unfaltering in his stubbornness to help even though his insides quaked. He'd never stood up to Noah before, never made demands or asked for special access to cases, but this was something Troy needed as much as oxygen.

He'd made a promise to Silas on the night of his arrest, and he would do whatever was necessary to see it through.

A few moments of silence and Noah exhaled loudly through his nose. "Fine. If you can't deny him, have at his arrogant ass—but you can't be actively involved in court. You'll help behind the scenes."

Noah had given him permission to fuck with their client, but doing so still meant Troy straddled a gray line, one he usually avoided crossing in all things.

"I won't let you or him down," Troy stated even though his internal war continued inside his head.

A hint of a smile lightened the intensity on Noah's face, and he clasped Troy's shoulder while moving past him. "You haven't yet—and we're both lucky to have you by our sides."

Troy's breath escaped in a rush, leaving him jittery and grinning. "Thank you, Noah."

Noah clasped his shoulder. "Just be careful."

"Always," Troy said and followed his boss from the office with determined steps.

It had been Noah's father who'd fought for him in court all those years ago, and even though Troy and his family had lost the case against his teacher, his hard work and dedication had earned their respect.

Being offered a position in Noah's new firm his father had helped him build had been a dream come true, and there wasn't anything Troy wouldn't do to prove his worth.

While he'd have preferred diving into Silas's case, he had other clients' folders on his desk. Unless Noah brought him on Silas's defense case full time, Troy would have to divide his work hours.

Not what he wanted to do, but his integrity demanded an equal sharing of his focus.

An hour later, the District Attorney's office called with discovery information. The secretary patched the assistant DA through to Troy since he'd informed her he would be working alongside Noah.

Troy didn't ask Greg Harlan for details about the reasons behind the arrest warrant a judge had signed. He promised to have Noah get in touch with him as soon as he was back from an off-site meeting.

A few minutes later, Noah passed by Troy's glass door, and Troy shot up from behind his desk and followed him.

"We received a call from the prosecutor regarding discovery," Troy said the second Noah shut them up in his office. "Call him back. I didn't ask for details." He hadn't meant for his words to come out so demanding, but he'd gotten caught up in the butterflies once more roused inside his stomach.

"I will, thank you."

Troy lingered, earning him a glance from Noah.

"Anything else?"

"Thank you again for allowing me to help with Silas's case."

"I trust you to keep your desires from interfering in any way. If your usual backbone of honesty is compromised, you need to come to me the second it begins to crumble. Understand?"

Troy felt confident of the ethical standards deeply ingrained in his mind, but would the tug of Silas on his heart create a battle he might lose? He hadn't been faced with that severe of temptation before where his livelihood could crumble beneath him. If Silas captivated his heart as easily as he had his body, would he walk shades of gray out of desire for the man regardless of Silas's innocence?

Ever since the event that changed his life had taken place, Troy had stuck to the moral high ground. He would continue to do so regardless of his emotions.

Knowing he got ahead of himself, Troy shook the thoughts from his mind. He ought to worry more about a being used and set aside by the known playboy.

But Troy couldn't think on that either.

"I understand, sir." Troy dipped his head in agreement to Noah's suggestion and scuttled from the room. He needed to concentrate on getting shit done so he could turn his attention to Silas's case.

The war of gray areas and sure broken hearts could wait.

After finishing up his work for the day and three hours of studying a few prominent self-defense cases won by Noah and his father, Troy's eyes ached. He sipped his fourth coffee of the afternoon while allowing himself a break to peer out his windows overlooking Boston's cityscape lit against the night sky. Tipped back in his office chair, he called his mom.

She always had a ready ear for her only son and acceptance in her heart no matter what he did or how he failed.

They exchanged their usual pleasantries before Troy spilled the story of the previous two weeks. From the moment he'd first seen Silas sitting in the holding room after the altercation to his present state of exhausted and stressed out, Troy gave her everything except the part about Silas getting on his knees and blowing his damn mind.

His mom chuckled.

Laughed.

Troy scowled. "This isn't funny, Mom."

"I know, darling, but I'm just thrilled to hear you've finally found a man who has your thoughts so wrapped up that you sound like a giddy teenager."

The last time that had happened, she'd been in the dark about the man's identity until shit went down, and they had all ended up in court.

Troy pushed aside memories of the past, refusing to give negativity a place in his mind. "I'm so worked up inside that I can't focus—"

"On anything but him," his mom interrupted, a smile evident in her tone.

"Yeah." Troy slumped, closing his eyes against the night sky in front of him. "Pretty much."

"It sounds to me like you've got some unfinished business with him."

"Mom," Troy groaned the word, embarrassment heating his face.

"I'm just saying, if that detective interrupted your first kiss—"

Troy had told a tiny white lie about the night Silas had been arrested.

"—then maybe you ought to go visit that man and finish what you started."

"Oh. My. God." Troy pinched the bridge of his nose, his empty coffee cup long since set aside.

"If Noah has given permission, then what's holding you back from exploring what might be the beginning of something beautiful?"

"A possible broken heart?"

"You listen to me, Troy Emerson," his mom stated firmly. "You deserve happiness. Love. Acceptance and honesty as much as you give. I know you have deep fears, lingering shit from that asshole, but you need to live. There's so much more to life than your job and proving yourself. You've already done that, and how you help others with your chosen work is admirable. But do *more*, son, do something for yourself. Take life by the balls and ride as long and as hard as you can."

Troy bit back another groan, muttering a curse in his head. Did his mom not realize how the words she so gently and lovingly stated sounded?

"I've got work to do," Troy said, suddenly sitting up and rolling his chair around to face his desk.

"I hope you mean you're going to go get that man and show him your sweet soul."

Troy wanted to show Silas a hell of a lot more than that but didn't respond other than to make a noise under his breath. He hoped he could stay on the proper side of right and wrong while doing so.

"Best of luck and I'll keep my fingers crossed for you," his mom said.

He didn't need either.

Silas was a sure thing—same as his mom would be to hold Troy when he showed up on her doorstep bleeding tears.

9

Silas

ilas's cell rang, pulling him from a deep, dreamless sleep. Annoyance sent a growl through his clenched jaw as he rolled to grab his phone from the bedside table.

He didn't recognize the number but knew without a doubt who had called. He'd already spoken with his sister earlier in the day to get caught up on the events since his arrest.

His scowl dissolved, and he settled back against his pillow with a smirk. "Tell me you're outside."

A shaky exhale filled his ear. "I'm outside," Troy whispered.

Silas hung up, yanked on a pair of boxer briefs, and hurried toward his front door. A glance through the peephole showed a flushed, delicious attorney waiting in the hallway.

Silas's heart stuttered, and he opened the door, his cocky grin fixed firmly in place.

Troy scowled at Silas's obvious *I told you so* painted on his face, but the dent in his forehead dissolved as his gaze slid down over Silas's almost naked form.

Blood rushed to Silas's groin, and his briefs tented. "Are you going to come in or just stand there and stare?"

The tip of Troy's tongue flitted over his lower lip, and Silas groaned, reaching for Troy's loosened tie and yanking him into the apartment before he could respond. A palm to the door slammed it shut, and Silas crowded Troy the same way he'd done on Friday night.

Every inch of Silas's skin burned as lust, hot and heavy, settled in his balls. Troy's clothes chafed at Silas's tight nipples as he held the boy's chin to the side, giving him access to his neck.

He inhaled and cursed over the scent of strawberries and vanilla filling his nose. "You smell so goddamn sweet."

Troy whimpered, and Silas slid his tongue from Troy's shirt's collar to his ear. "Delicious," he whispered and nipped at his lobe, dick throbbing at Troy's shudder. "I want to taste every goddamn inch of your luscious skin."

"Yes, please and thank you," Troy all but begged.

Silas stepped back suddenly, leaving Troy swaying. He laced his fingers through Troy's and led him toward the bedroom they hadn't made it to before.

"Take off all your clothes," Silas told him, "so I can see how badly you want my dick."

Troy didn't argue but stood at the foot of Silas's bed and started to strip, his hands shaking while ripping his tie free from around his neck.

The last time Silas had stood on the verge of enjoying every fucking inch of the irresistible young man, they'd been interrupted. But there was nothing on the planet that would stop the fall ahead of him. No self-preservation, no worries of the future, and certainly no damn police.

Troy set his tie on the edge of Silas's bed rather than dropping it to the floor.

Satisfaction coursed through him at the knowledge that Troy had noted Silas's inclination toward neat and orderly.

"Good boy," Silas said with a wink, holding up his hand when Troy opened his mouth to doubtless argue his word choice. "Be right back."

He hurried to his bathroom for a quick swish of mouthwash, his erection staying at the ready and leading the way on his return to the bedroom.

Silas's steps pulled up short at the sight awaiting him.

Troy had listened to Silas's command, his clothes

nicely folded and set on the foot of the bed when he'd expected them to be in a pile of the floor. He bent, lining up his shoes beneath the bed's foot.

A gorgeous flush rose over his chest and cheeks as he straightened and faced Silas, an ethereal glow about him beneath the bedroom's dimmed overheads.

Pale skin from head to bare toes made Silas's fingers itch to touch. A freckle beside his furled left nipple beckoned to Silas's tongue. Troy's narrow waist showcased prominent hip bones Silas salivated to lick. Bite.

And the waxed groin he remembered the musky scent of, the slender cock he lusted to taste again…

Silas groaned, his balls tightening. "My little elfin angel, what a beautiful vision you are."

Troy's mouth worked like he wanted to argue Silas's possessive word again and the description he'd given. The good boy didn't speak when Silas moved around him without caressing an inch of his skin.

Silas retrieved lube and condoms from the bedside table and tossed them atop his mattress. He returned to stand in front of Troy—too far away but close enough to touch. He once more slid his gaze down over the expanse of smooth skin covering valleys and bulges, the most alluring of which reached upward almost to Troy's belly button.

While Silas's mouth watered for another taste, he needed more than cum on his tongue.

He shoved down his boxer briefs and stepped forward, taking Troy's parted lips in a bruising kiss. The heated sexual tension erupted to boiling within a single heartbeat. Skin on skin, from lips to knees, they ground together, moans and gasps mingling in the silence enclosing them in a world of their own.

Troy tasted like strawberries and sunshine, and Silas couldn't get enough.

Pre-cum smeared between their dicks, easing the rutting that tightened Silas's balls up against his body. He palmed Troy's pert ass cheeks, kneading. Squeezing with every thrust of his groin against Troy's.

"Silas," Troy whispered, shaking in his arms and clutching at his shoulders as though he was as desperate as Silas felt.

Silas had never known such need before. None of the women he'd fucked had taken him to the point he felt mad with lust.

Gritting his teeth to stay in control, Silas slid a dry finger down the top of Troy's crack, reaching for soft, puckered skin.

Troy let out a whimper and widened his stance, opening to Silas's touch.

Slickness waited for him.

"Fuck," Silas groaned, his entire core going tight with the instinct to claim.

"I didn't want to waste any time—"

"*Naughty* boy. It looks like that feast I had planned will have to wait." Silas stepped away, spun Troy, and pressed him forward. "Chest on the bed," he growled, his insides quivering.

Troy went willingly, arching his back and giving Silas another view to die for.

His pink, puckered asshole smeared with lube, ready for Silas's dick.

It wasn't the first one Silas had been faced with, wouldn't be the first he had wrecked, but he knew without doubt it would be the most fulfilling. Too many addictive emotions swarmed inside his chest for Troy to be a mere fuck, a hole to offer release.

Silas stared a moment longer while tugging down on his balls to take him off the edge of ejaculating like a pubescent teen. Once more in control, he grasped Troy's cheeks, spreading him wider, groaning at the thought of thrusting inside the boy's tight heat. "So pretty. I'm going to fill you up so damn good, angel."

"Silas," Troy moaned and shifted his hips. "Just give me your dick already."

Chuckling, Silas grabbed the condom and lube. His hands shook while he sheathed up and smeared slickness down his length. Troy might have prepped before coming to him, but the more lube, the better.

He slid a finger over Troy's hole, tip gently probing with teasing thrusts. The wet sounds of

Troy's ass attempting to suck Silas's finger inside tightened his ball sack back up against his groin.

Another moan escaped Troy, and Silas pressed—easily sliding his finger fully into Troy's body. His cock jolted, and a hiss leaked from his parted lips.

"Your ass is so fucking tight." Silas twisted his wrist, feeling along the silken walls clasped around his finger. "Christ, are you hot. Can't wait to feel your ass choking my cock."

"Please," Troy begged, and Silas found his prostate. "Oh fuck…" Troy arched his back deeper.

"Don't come." Silas rubbed again.

A strangled noise choked from Troy's throat as he fisted the sheets. "Please…"

Silas gave him a second finger while once more tugging down on his balls.

The tight ring of Troy's ass clutched at his probing, and Silas scissored his fingers, earning whimpers and gasps.

"I'm ready for you," Troy whined.

"Just don't want to hurt you," Silas said through gritted teeth since edging the boy ramped him up to the same degree of wanting to beg.

Troy lifted his head from the mattress and turned to look over his shoulder. Lust hazed his blue eyes, swelling his pupils. "I *want* you to hurt me—I-I just need to see you when you do it."

"Fuck." Silas pulled out his fingers, grabbed hold of his cheeks, and spread him wide enough that Troy whimpered. Silas trembled, stood on the goddamn edge of some unknown he couldn't name but craved with an intensity that stole his breath. "Exhale and let me in…"

Silas shoved his cock deep with one thrust, pulling groans from both their lungs. Tightness clasped at his length, swallowing him whole without resistance. He bottomed out in exquisite, silken heat.

"Oh shit…shit," Troy groaned, his widened eyes on Silas's.

"Okay?"

Their gazes held, Silas damn near blinded by the burning perfection of Troy's ass.

"Mmm." Troy mangled the noise but nodded.

Silas dragged out slowly, hissing as Troy constricted his muscle stretched around Silas's girth.

Forget angel—Troy Emerson was the devil incarnate.

Silas slammed into him again, sliding Troy forward on the bed until his hips hit the mattress and he cried out at the brute force. "You want it to hurt?"

"Yes—please." He gasped as Silas plowed into him again. "Talk to me. Need to hear your voice if I can't see you."

A red flag flickered briefly in Silas's brain, but there was no way he could stop what had finally started.

They were an iridescent nebula on the verge of detonation.

"You feel so *fucking* good. Hot. Tight." Silas thrust into Troy over and over, words of praise and curses spilling from his lips while he gave Troy what he'd asked for. He'd never owned an ass like he did Troy's, and fuck, how he wished to spurt his cum deep inside. Watch it dribble out in oozing globs of white he could shove back in.

Next time, he promised himself and pulled out fully.

Troy's whimper cut off as Silas hauled him up onto the bed and sank balls deep into his tight hole again. "Christ, Troy, your ass is heaven."

Silas's hand to Troy's shoulder blades sent his chest to the mattress, but he couldn't remain upright as Silas continued to rail into him over and over. Steady, violent thrusts filled the bedroom with the sounds of slapping skin.

"I want to fuck you all night long." Curses spilled from Silas's lips as he continued to pound into Troy. "You take me so. Fucking. Good."

Troy's body slid forward along the mattress with each grunted word, and Silas followed, blanketing the younger man with his sweat-slickened body. Silas's heart thundered against Troy's back, his hot, panted exhales over his ear.

He slid an arm beneath Troy's chest and took his throat in hand. "This okay?"

Troy whimpered but rasped an affirmative. "J-Just talk to me."

"Always. Hold on, angel. Let me have it all."

Troy melted beneath his grasp in clear, beautiful submission.

10

Troy

For the first time since *him*, Troy gave himself fully to a man. Offered up his body, and Silas took, his grip on Troy's throat tightening enough that he moaned, uncaring if he passed out from the lack of oxygen.

And he hadn't even needed vodka to cross that line. He craved Silas's touch, felt oddly...*safe* in his hold. Any psychiatrist would have a field day with his past and present situation, the way he willingly gave into lust, but Troy didn't question.

He just existed in that moment...and it was *damn* good as Silas whispered nasty shit against his ear, licking and nibbling his neck between words.

Silas's hip bones bruised against his backside with every thrust, the jabs of his length rubbing over his prostate time and again, smearing pre-cum all over the comforter beneath Troy.

His balls were going to erupt.

With devastating force.

A whine built up in Troy's throat with the tingles at the base of his spine. "Holy *fucking* shit, I'm going to come so hard."

"Give it to me," Silas demanded.

"Silas—" Troy choked out and shuddered as the first wave of pleasure slammed into him.

"Jesus. Fuck." Silas sat back, using his hold on Troy's throat to pull him against his chest. He wrapped his free hand around Troy's pulsing dick and thrust deep into his spasming ass.

Ropes of cum shot over Silas's bed, and Troy cried out, reaching behind him to grab hold of Silas's head. His back arched in desperation to take Silas deeper.

"Yes…fuck." Silas held his throat, pumping with his other fist in time with his pistoning hips until Troy's balls ran dry. "Christ, angel." Silas gasped against his ear as Troy went boneless. "You felt so fucking good coming around my dick. Fuck. Want to fill you full of my cum…."

Silas shuddered against Troy's back, and he slammed in deep, his dick pulsing his release inside the condom.

Troy wanted what Silas had groaned, imagined every grunt and short thrust from Silas flooding his ass with wet heat.

One last tremor, and Silas went still, clutching at

Troy, holding him tight against his chest. They both panted, the sounds of their ragged breaths barely reaching through the ringing in Troy's ears.

He'd never come so hard in his life, and he gulped in oxygen, wanting to be choked out again. "That was…" A shiver slid over him, pebbling his sweaty skin.

"Mmm." Silas nuzzled his neck, his ear, his hot breath keeping the goosebumps in place. "Sweet, delicious boy."

"Not a boy," Troy argued without any heat in his tone and a smile on his lips, unlike how he'd wanted to declare earlier.

Silas roamed his mouth to where Troy's neck met his shoulder, and he clamped on, sucking.

Troy rolled his head to the side for the marking.

No one but he and Silas would see it—and he wanted the memory of their night together in the event Silas had satisfied his curiosity about dick.

The reality of what Troy had allowed settled in and roiled nausea in his guts. He'd asked for Silas to hurt him, had willingly submitted to the dominant hold on his neck.

An ache ripped through Troy's chest at both thoughts, and Silas backed out, taking his dick with him at the same time.

Troy moaned at the sudden emptiness, the cold along his back, but Silas gently laid him down, away from the cum splattered over the bed.

Silas planked over his sprawled body and nipped at his lower lip. "Okay?" Concern filled his eyes, which caused Troy's throat to tighten.

He nodded. Silas was not *him*—far fucking from it.

"Be right back." Silas pecked his lips before crawling off the bed. His voice promised he wasn't ready to kick Troy out, so he pushed aside that fear as well. Relaxation came, zero memories or stirred up trauma invading his thoughts like he had expected.

The sound of running water reached Troy's ears, but he couldn't hold his eyelids open. Exhaustion rose like a swelling tidal wave, ready to crash on the shore of Troy's mind.

Wetness wiped between his splayed thighs, keeping him from sliding fully into sleep. Silas held his knee, lifting higher, giving him access to clean Troy's ass.

He made a noise of approval deep in his throat. "Red and raw…you're going to feel me for days."

"Good," Troy murmured sleepily, his eyelids falling shut again.

The soft touch of a gentle kiss on his wrecked hole jerked his eyes open.

Silas's dark head dipped between his legs, and he kissed it again. His tongue flicked out, and Troy groaned, his need for sleep ready to take a back seat.

Silas chuckled and kissed the inside of his thigh,

his spent dick that wanted to wake up but couldn't, his lower abs, and atop his heart before finally reaching Troy's mouth. "Stay with me tonight?" Silas whispered across Troy's lips.

The question rather than a command or assumption warmed Troy in deeper parts than their fucking had touched. He cradled Silas's face and studied him in the dim light.

Vulnerability shone in hazel eyes normally shut off from any emotion except for lust.

Troy's heart skipped a beat, and he had to force down rising hope. "Okay."

Silas rolled him even farther from the cum stains, wrapping them up beneath the massive bed's comforter in a warm cocoon. He cradled Troy's back to his chest as the big spoon and nuzzled his nape. "Sleep, angel."

Troy did without further prompting.

A cell's notification ring registered in Troy's mind, but it was Silas cursing and rolling away from him that brought him fully awake. Too tired, too sore to move, Troy lay still, his eyelids heavy and closed.

"The fuck?" Silas whispered harshly and shifted but didn't leave the bed. He went silent for a few moments.

Another incoming text dinged in the quiet.

Quiet ringing sounded, and a feminine voice answered Silas's call.

"You never told me the reason you weren't staying at the house was anything to do with fear, Grace. Are you having a hard time?" Silas whispered.

Troy pretended to still be passed out when he should have given Silas privacy to speak with his sister.

She spoke again, the words unclear.

"I have company that is sleeping," Silas told her, his voice low, "and I don't want to startle them awake. Promise me you will tell me if things are too much and you need me, okay?"

Troy's chest ached at the softness in Silas's voice even though he'd given her a command. His younger sister brought out a side of Silas that Troy had yet to see.

A very sweet one. Gentle.

"I love you, Grace."

God, those words. To have someone other than a parent speak them with such adamant adoration…

Troy's throat tightened, and he allowed himself to fantasize about hearing that same thing, those same inflections, from the sexy man who returned to snuggle against his back.

Hardness gliding up through his wet ass crack brought Troy back to reality, and it took all of three seconds for him to recognize the Boston skyline backlit by the rising sun in the windows he faced.

Silas's hands roamed over his front while he gyrated his hips again, sliding his dick between Troy's ass cheeks. He'd already slickened his dick and was getting himself off.

Arching his back, Troy offered himself with a shuddered sigh. What a way to wake up…

"I want you," Silas growled against his ear while lifting Troy's thigh to drape over his.

"Condom," Troy whispered.

"Already on," Silas replied and shifted to notch the head of his dick. One slow push and he slid halfway into Troy's sore hole.

"Oh *fuck*." Troy hissed at the pain, gritting his teeth.

Silas pinched his nipple and bit his earlobe while pulling out a bit. "Relax and let me in, Mr. Emerson."

"God, yes, please." Troy groaned the words as Silas pressed back in. He shuddered and breathed through the sting as Silas filled him and held still. Balls deep, his hard body wrapped around Troy's.

"So hot and tight." Silas's words heated Troy's ear. "You take me so fucking perfectly." He gathered Troy's flaccid dick in hand and toyed with him, tugging on his length and caressing his balls, all while buried and unmoving in his ass.

Silas spit on his palm and returned to Troy's semi, the slickness creating an enticing friction.

Troy's backside adjusted to the intrusion, his dick going hard in Silas's hold.

"Mmm," Silas murmured against his ear. "Much better." He began rocking against Troy's backside, gently stroking in and out of his ass in time with his hand.

Nothing about his slow, sweet movements suggested a mere hookup, and Troy's heart swelled with longing—and even more fear than the evening before.

"I've never let someone stay the night," Silas proclaimed, still moving deep inside Troy with slow, toe-curling drags of his hard cock. "Never."

"I feel special," Troy half-snarked, going along with Silas's lovemaking, fucking himself onto his dick and into his fist.

"You should—you are." Silas turned Troy's head and took his mouth, morning breath be damned.

Troy arched his back so Silas could sink deeper, whimpering over his mouth as his balls tightened up against his body. "Fuck, Silas…"

"Yeah, angel. You feel so fucking good. Love this ass." He buried deep and bit down on Troy's lower lip.

Troy couldn't help the smile beneath Silas's kisses and nibbles. Silas had claimed he'd never been with a guy before, but there was no denying he liked Troy's dick. Every welled pearl of pre-cum Silas enticed from Troy brought a rumbled groan of approval from his chest as he slid it over Troy's length.

"Love how you leak for me." Silas pushed fully into Troy's ass and released his cock.

Troy whimpered, grabbing at Silas's wrist to put it on his throbbing dick, but Silas proved stronger—and brought his hand to his mouth, his tongue taking a long drag upward through the stickiness on his palm.

A spine-tingling groan rumbled against Troy's back, Silas's dick jolting deep inside him.

"So damn delicious. *Fuck.*" Silas grabbed Troy's hip, pulling out and slamming inside, control lost. Two harsh thrusts and he came, cursing and fingertips bruising Troy's skin.

"Silas…" Balls aching, Troy grabbed his dick, desperate for release.

"Nuh uh." Silas pulled out and flipped Troy onto his back, swallowing him down.

Within seconds of Silas's mouth sucking on his length, cum erupted from Troy's balls with a shit ton of emotion he couldn't deny.

He was falling for Silas, good and truly fucked should things go bad between them—or in court.

11

Silas

Silas hadn't lied to Troy. He'd never allowed a hookup to sleep in his bed, but a storm of possessiveness had owned him when Troy came all over his comforter as though marking Silas's bed as his.

Rarely did Silas allow himself to let go fully, to take what he lusted for, exactly how he wanted it, but Troy had welcomed the rough handling, the ruthless, near brutal thrusts as Silas had fucked him the evening before.

Silas leaned against his counter drinking coffee, his gaze on Troy's blue eyes peering at him from a few feet away where he stood, wondering over that red flag he'd taken note of while fucking the boy.

Had there been more to Troy's story about his teacher that Chávez had unearthed? Had he been forced, held down against his will? Such trauma would definitely make a person have triggers like Troy's.

Anger burned hot in Silas's gut, but he tamped it deep, saving the rage for another day.

They'd shared a beautiful night together, and Silas wasn't about to stir shit up. Yes, he wanted to know Troy inside and out, his every thought, every memory. Wanted to eventually lay claim to every goddamn piece of the delicious man.

But for now, he would just enjoy whatever had begun between them and hope Troy would eventually open up to him in the future.

Troy held a mug in his hands, a soft smile on his lips, clueless to the thoughts flitting through Silas's head.

They'd showered together after Silas had woken him with an early morning gift of his dick. He'd never shot off so damn easily, so unexpectedly, but the tight heat of Troy's body around his dick, the taste of his pre-cum on Silas's palm...

He'd ejaculated like a kid getting his first taste of pussy.

Pussy.

Silas's gaze flitted down over Troy's body, the smooth, hairless skin, a hint of pectoral muscles, and flat, dark nipples. A lean torso with bumped abs led southward to pink lace panties that cupped Troy's bulge.

Fucking panties.

On a man.

Lust stirred Silas's groin, and he sipped his coffee, gaze continuing down over Troy's thighs and the light dusting of hair—the same strawberry blond atop his head. Shapely calf muscles, far from feminine feet, and toenails without a bit of painted color.

Completely masculine yet beautiful.

"What are you thinking?"

Silas lifted his focus back up to find Troy studying his face. "That you're the most stunning man I've ever seen."

"I'm wearing panties—lace—and you're just now seeing me as a man rather than a boy or kid?"

Smirking, Silas shrugged. "Calling you boy and kid is a newfound favorite kink. Besides, I like to tease."

"You're good at it."

"I'm good at a lot of things." Silas couldn't contain his smug grin.

Troy slid his gaze down over Silas as slowly as Silas had done to him, making a noise of approval in his throat before sipping his coffee.

"What are *you* thinking?" Silas asked.

"That a boy like me could get too tangled up in you and end up brokenhearted."

Troy's blunt honesty hit hard but shouldn't have surprised Silas. Wariness didn't stab at Silas's mind—he trusted Troy. His integrity kept a strong hold on his actions except when it came to Silas.

"I'm feeling the same," he admitted, ready for more true words between them.

Their gazes locked as silence settled.

It was too soon for such discussions, Silas knew, but masculinity and lack of pussy aside, Troy had captured his full attention in such a way that he didn't question their attraction or the chemistry that had ignited between them in his bed.

He also didn't need to examine his desire for Troy, more mornings of exchanging sleepy kisses and gentle lovemaking.

It hadn't been mere fucking as the sun had risen to hit Silas's bedroom with stark, bright reality. Their giving and receiving had involved a lot of emotion, leaving behind a feeling of contentment Silas hadn't ever experienced before.

His chest ached for Troy, and his soul craved to love on him over and over again.

Silas didn't need a label to explain what he and Troy had started. The younger man fit him like a goddamn glove, and he would do anything to keep such a possession.

If Troy wanted him regardless of truth or lies. Perhaps it wasn't too soon to ask...at least one thing would be settled in his life.

"I have to go to work," Troy broke eye contact and the chance for more discussion between them, setting his mug aside.

A heavy exhale deflated Silas's lungs.

"Same—but you'll be at the conference on Wednesday?" Silas hadn't expected to sound so damn needy, but he didn't care that his hope bled into every word.

"I'm not able to actively defend you, but like I promised, I'll be by your side, seeing you through to the end."

Silas prayed there wouldn't be an end to *them*.

Silas sat with Noah and Troy, going over the case for the first time as a team. He'd already shared his story with them individually, but Noah dropped the discovery he'd been called with on Monday, the reasons behind the warrant.

While Silas explained both, too damn aware of the angel on his left, he kept parts of the truth to himself. Especially the shit that would draw his little sister into the case. Silas knew things about her he didn't want unearthed—for her safety and her reputation. But some of what would doubtless come out during the trial would piss her the hell off.

His sister would forgive him in the end.

She always did.

"I can't make promises, but with what you've told us this morning," Noah stated, "I think the prosecution will do more damage for themselves if they call her as a witness. Now…" He moved some papers on his desk, his eyebrows furrowing. "I expect they'll offer a lesser charge and sentence in exchange—"

"No." Silas's tone and expression were as firm as his gaze on his lawyer. "It was self-defense. I didn't—"

Noah held up his hand, cutting off his claim of innocence. "I don't want to know. I won't ever ask. There's some serious circumstantial evidence here. If we can't discredit witnesses and the prosecution team ends up with a jury inclined to believe them—"

"I have a guy." Silas's interruption pulled Noah's focus off the file in front of him.

"A guy?" Troy asked.

"Private investigator." Silas enjoyed the excuse to look at his lover before glancing back at Noah. "If you need shit on someone, he's your man. He's thorough, fast, and has connections in all the right shady places."

"Credentials?" Noah requested, and Silas filled him in, having asked for them years earlier before hiring the man himself.

Noah slowly nodded as Troy took down the information Silas provided.

"So he'll go about gathering the type of evidence we need without breaking the law," Noah said. "I could call him as a witness if need be."

"Absolutely," Silas stated with assurance and handed over Chávez's personal information. While Noah jotted down the PI's number, Silas turned his focus on Troy. The few feet separating them felt more like a massive chasm, but warmth and desire welled up inside Silas regardless of the distance.

Troy emanated…*something* that drew Silas toward him.

He didn't hate the feelings, but he wanted to bathe in the emotions rising up inside him, stand beneath whatever it was while it rained over his head, down his entire body. Troy's steady gaze suggested the same, full of heat and longing. Blood stirred in Silas's groin regardless of where they sat and the reason for their meeting.

But what if things went terribly wrong? What if the prosecution team somehow managed to make circumstantial shit look like solid evidence—enough to put him away for the better part of his life?

His stomach twisted, but he kept his face unmoved. He only allowed Troy to see the longing, the desire for more with him.

"You two…" Noah cursed, slapping his pen onto his desk and standing. "Don't make me regret my decision to allow you on this case, Mr. Emerson."

Troy swallowed audibly, tearing his focus off Silas and leaving him with an inner emptiness atop the anxiety churning Silas's guts. "I won't let you down, sir."

A bailiff announced the judge was ready for them, and Silas followed Noah and Troy into the conference room where the prosecution team already awaited their arrival. Adrenaline leaked through his bloodstream, but Silas kept in control. Shoulders back, chin lifted, he knew he appeared cocky and confident as always.

Greg Harlan, the assistant District Attorney had been at Silas's arraignment, but he hadn't given the lawyer more than a glance.

Their gazes met, and Silas dipped his head in acknowledgement.

Greg ignored him, but he wasn't surprised. Noah had told him the man was an arrogant ass.

Troy sat beside Silas—but not nearly close enough. He wanted to lean against his boy, be the one cradled in warm, soothing arms.

Silas had thought he knew what fear was, but being faced with a greater loss than freedom, kept him on edge, barely managing to stay focused and still.

As expected, the District Attorney's office offered a lesser sentence if Silas pleaded guilty, and as directed, Noah declined.

The pre-trial was set for almost four weeks' time.

Only twenty-eight days, not nearly enough for all Silas wanted to do with Troy. He had plans, big ones, that included showing him the world, spending hours talking about useless shit, snuggling beneath blankets every morning as though each day was a weekend. Breakfast in bed. Hearing his whimpers and gasps as he came for Silas.

The judge cleared his throat, pulling Silas's attention back to the conference room.

"I expect to have witness lists in my hands by the end of the day," he stated, a no-nonsense man whose poker face matched Silas's.

"They're already completed, Your Honor." Greg offered a file, a smug smirk on his lips.

Silas had learned their supposed evidence and trusted his PI to get the job done as he had dozens of times before.

Silas returned the assistant DA's confident look with one of his own even though his insides twisted with worry.

The judge stood, and everyone around the table joined him, waiting until he left the room to make any further moves.

Greg Harlan exchanged a few words with his team, but Silas didn't give him the time of day before following Noah out the door. The hairs on his nape tingled, but when it came to Troy on his heels, there wasn't a part of him that didn't take note of his presence.

He wanted to twine his fingers with Troy's, show the world what he'd found, what he had every intention of keeping—if the jury allowed such a future.

Noah would shit his pants if Silas openly claimed his young lover.

Such acts of possessiveness ought to wait until he was cleared of all charges, but Silas found his stubbornness, his selfishness, rising to the surface as always.

He'd found something beautiful, unexpected, and mind-consuming.

Why waste time instead of taking what you wanted—especially since it might only be a total of four weeks?

Life was too goddamn short for black and white, and he'd always preferred shades of grey anyway.

12

Troy

Troy spent more time at Silas's place than he did his own, waking to Boston's skyline and a hot mouth on his body, worshiping his smooth skin like Silas had said he wanted to do.

Silas claimed Troy was a sweet addiction he couldn't get enough of. Every day sitting in his office, Troy daydreamed of Silas's hands on him, being kissed and bitten by the man's sensual mouth. Purple marks littered Troy's chest and shoulders, and that morning, Silas had decided to spread the hickeys further down Troy's body, sucking and nibbling on his inner thighs.

They'd spent the better part of the following workweek stealing moments when able to, but they had to fight off the need to touch whenever Silas came into Noah's office.

Friday night, Troy gladly skipped out on *Posh* for

the second week in a row, having agreed to a first real date with Silas. As always, the man overindulged, showing off his money and status.

They went to a swanky joint Troy would never be able to afford on his salary, the type of place you couldn't event reserve a seat unless you were *someone*.

The hostess had greeted Silas by name before taking them to a secluded table near the back of the intimate restaurant. The dimmed lighting and muffled instrumental music from overhead speakers created a bubble-like, sensual atmosphere.

And the way Silas stared at him, inspecting every inch of Troy's body he could see above the linen-covered table between them kept Troy half-hard. Troy knew Silas's reputation, had heard he was never seen out with a woman more than once.

He could get whomever he wanted, then discarded the poor souls once he'd sampled the goods.

At least, that was what people said.

But he'd only ever been seen out with women.

"So have you always been bi?" Troy asked while slicing a scallop in half. Some sort of creamy, lemon sauce slathered over the succulent bites. The seafood melted on his tongue.

Silas watched him suck the fork clean on the way out of his mouth before he chewed. His eyes darkened when his gaze lifted to Troy's. "I'm not a fan of labels, but if being attracted to just one man ever —*you*—then I guess that's what you'd call me."

Troy swallowed a groan along with his mouthful of food. "You've never wanted to fuck a man before?"

"Never even considered it."

Troy smirked and licked his fork again.

"Tease."

"Mmm."

Silas grinned and returned to his steak. "I don't know what it is about you, Mr. Emerson, but the second you walked into the holding room, I knew I had to have you. I went hard as nails within seconds."

"And it didn't bother you that I didn't have your preferred bits hidden in my panties?"

Silas let out a low growl and lifted an eyebrow, a promise in his gaze. "I like your dick—and I love seeing it wrapped up in lace and silk."

"So I noticed." Troy softly snicker. "I would go so far as to say you might even be addicted to it."

"That wouldn't be a lie."

A thrill shot through Troy, creating flutters in his belly. "This is the third time you've been seen in public with me. Aren't you afraid people might start talking?"

Silas chewed a bite of steak, studying him in that way that always made Troy wonder what went through his head. He swallowed down his food with a sip of red wine. "Doesn't that box you put me in include the personality trait of *I-doesn't-have-any-fucks-to-give* when it comes to people judging me?"

Oh, to be so confident. "You really don't care what people think or say about you?"

"I care what *you* think about me."

A slow smile lifted Troy's lips, drawing Silas's focus.

"Tell me," Silas demanded, his gaze on Troy's mouth.

Troy flicked out his tongue over his lower lip. "Where to begin." His voice came out breathless, partly intentional, but the main drive behind his suggestive tone was his thickening length.

"While your confidence should be off-putting, I find it strangely…enticing," Troy began. "The width of your shoulders, your height, should intimidate me, but I like our size difference. Your drive to get what you want is sexy as hell. Your loyalty to family, your generosity outside the spotlight intrigues the fuck out of me. I believe there's a softer side to Silas Barlowe—and I get hints of that delicious part of you every morning when your hands are gentle and your kisses are sleepy and warm."

"I'm not a romantic."

Troy huffed a snort. "I beg to differ. I've seen that hidden part of you. Felt it just this morning when you took your sweet time worshiping every inch of my body. If you want my honesty, I think I've brought that side of you out—same as I made you gay for me."

"Gay for you." Silas seemed to consider the words while swirling the last of his wine in his glass. "That sounds more appropriate than bisexual."

Flutters awakened in Troy's stomach again. It would be too damn easy to fall for Silas. And what would happen once Silas had his fill of exploring with the same sex? Would Troy be set aside, the heart he'd willingly given shattered to pieces?

Troy had experienced that type of pain once before and had no wish to wallow in depression again. It was bad enough that memories of his old trauma oftentimes messed up sexual encounters. He didn't need another ex to jade his heart completely.

As long as Troy kept his focus on Silas and the filthy words pouring from his lips, Troy had no problems staying present with the sexy man. But a soul cracked open by Silas who seemed to fit him in every way, would ruin him for life.

His serious thoughts must have shown on his face, because Silas peered at him in the restaurant's dim light.

"What are you thinking?" Troy asked his new favorite question whenever he caught Silas studying him like he tried to understand the workings of the universe. He didn't mean to fish but found himself too curious about Silas's processing.

He knew Silas's body from head to pinkie toe,

had kissed and sucked on every inch of his flesh, but had yet to figure out his mind.

And he wanted to. Desperately.

Regardless of the fear such thoughts brought to life inside his head and heart.

Silas's gaze lightened as though he pushed seriousness to a back burner for later.

"I'm thinking—" he licked over his lower lip then smirked at Troy's whispered moan "—that I want to hold your hand when we leave. Tuck you in close against my body to let every person here and outside know who you're with."

Shivers licked over Troy's skin, and he took his time folding his napkin before placing it on the table. That hadn't been what Troy expected Silas to say. He'd anticipated something sexual, a blunt statement about Silas burying his dick in Troy's ass and wringing every drop of cum from both their balls.

No, Silas's words sounded…sweetly possessive, like a soul-deep longing that went beyond the physical. The same desire resonated in Troy's chest.

If only he could allow himself to trust the feeling —trust Silas.

"Then do it," Troy whispered, knowing he'd crossed a gray line—but he couldn't find it in himself to care. Or feel guilty.

"What about fraternizing with a client?" Silas asked quietly, still studying Troy's face.

"I'm not the one actively defending you in court."

A truth even if doing so wasn't exactly proper in their situation. Troy lifted his chin as though stating his case. "There's no law against us."

Silas's eyes burned with heat, but the arrival of their waiter paused their conversation. Silas took care of the bill, then gave Troy his full attention. "My sweet angel knows how to straddle the black-and-white line. I like it." He flashed a groin-aching grin, got up from his chair, and held out his hand. "Shall we?"

Troy twined their fingers together and stood, a sense of belonging and rightness swooping down over him, bringing back his inner jitters as they strolled from the restaurant. Silas held the door open like a true gentleman but snagged Troy's hand immediately afterward again, pulling him in close like he'd said he wanted to do.

Pausing on the sidewalk, Troy filled his lungs, trying to tamp down his giddiness. If he'd had vodka rather than wine, giggles would have probably burst from his lips.

He gazed up at his lover, knowing hearts shone in his eyes. "Silas—"

The squeal of tires cut Troy off, loud pops hitting his ears. Silas shoved—and Troy fell as screams filled the air.

His back connected with the ground, the air ripped from his lungs with a harsh *oomph!* as Silas landed atop him.

More pops.

A woman shrieking in hysterics.

Breathe…Troy couldn't breathe…

"Fuck!" Silas cursed, his head whipping around while plastered on top of Troy.

"Get down!" A man hollered.

Two more loud bangs, and glass shattered from above them.

Silas cursed and seemed to make himself wider, like an umbrella, catching the raining shards from hitting Troy.

Truth of what transpired kicked into Troy's brain, and he went light-headed, still struggling to fully inhale.

A drive-by shooting…gunshots.

Adrenaline shot through him like a bullet, allowing a lungful of oxygen and causing his pulse to race.

An engine roared, fading into the distance while the ruckus of shouts and screams continued around them.

Tremors pumped through Troy with every beat of his heart, and an involuntary childish whimper escaped him as he clutched at Silas's sides.

"Troy." Silas lifted off him enough to check Troy, his hands roaming over his face, his neck. Stark fear filled Silas's eyes. The frantic yet soft touch comforted him and caused Troy's eyes to prickle with tears.

"I-I'm okay," he gasped out.

"Fucking hell." Silas shifted onto his knees, quickly searching over Troy's body with shaking hands, the concern still etched in the grooves of his face.

Seeing the man on the verge of losing his shit, his control shattered, brought forth Troy's need to assure, to protect him.

"Silas." Troy pushed upright, grabbing Silas's wrists with his own shaking hands to calm his frantic movements. "I'm alright—not hurt. You?"

Silas swallowed hard and nodded before grabbing Troy in a tight hug. "Goddamnit, angel…if you'd been hit. Fuck." Silas's voice cracked and shuddered, and he swallowed convulsively as though to keep from sobbing.

Once more, Troy couldn't breathe, but he burrowed closer against Silas's hard chest, reveling in the thrumming thumb beneath his ear. The warmth and subtle scent of Silas's cologne swarmed his senses, and he clung to the man for dear life.

He'd never had someone care so much for his wellbeing outside his parents. His throat swelled, his own heart ready to burst. Words wanted to pour from his lips, but he bit the lower one to keep them for a better time.

Troy closed his eyes, soaking in the moment of surprising peace—a sense of rightness—since hell doubtless waited on the heels of whatever the fuck had just occurred.

Hours and countless interviews with law enforcement later, they hadn't learned anything more than they'd seen and heard.

While Troy hadn't taken note of the vehicle or single occupant shooting from the driver's window, Silas had.

Dark sedan, masked gunman with a Glock, no license plate.

Other witnesses in the area were also questioned, but the lead detective told Silas and Troy they didn't have much to go on. With a promise to find the shooter who hadn't managed to land a single shot into flesh, the detective finally allowed them to leave.

Two in the morning, and Troy didn't argue as Silas drove them straight to his place rather than offering to take Troy home.

Troy's insides still twisted up as tight as their clasped hands atop his thigh. Silas had clung to him with adamant possessiveness the entire night, only allowing them to be separated for questioning.

While Troy should have been settled by the blatant display of protectiveness, worry ate at his overstimulated mind.

He didn't doubt that he had fallen in love with Silas Barlowe. His every thought, every action, revolved around the man who'd stormed into his life uninvited, occupying and making his presence known in every cell of Troy's body.

Perhaps it was time to share the pieces of him his past had caused him to become. The reason for his honesty, his integrity. Keeping the truth from Silas seemed like a lie, and if they had a future ahead of them, his lover deserved to know.

But would Silas look at him in a different light? Would he believe what hundreds of others hadn't?

Fear sneaked its way into his heart and mind, soiling the sense of rightness he'd experienced throughout their date. He wanted to cling to the warm fuzzies he'd felt in the aftereffects of the shooting, but trust in the man who'd stolen his heart wavered.

Restlessness ate at his insides, and Troy questioned the hand grasping his as Silas drove him home. Cold crept through his limbs regardless of Silas's gentle touches of assurance on his lower back as the elevator took them to the top floor. He wiped dampened palms down his pants.

Troy wasn't sure he could survive having yet another loved one think he lied.

"What's on your mind, angel?" Silas murmured against Troy's hair. "I can hear the gears grinding inside your head."

They snuggled in bed, freshly showered, Silas the big spoon as usual. The warmth of the hard chest against Troy's back comforted in a way he'd never felt with anyone but Silas.

But the clenching in his stomach kept him from relaxing.

He wanted to cling to that sense of belonging and safety. Grasp hold of Silas's acceptance and never let go like he'd done after the shooting, but…

"Troy."

Exhaling loudly, Troy closed his eyes, shutting out Silas's dimmed bedroom that felt more like home than his rented one.

"When I was a senior in high school…" Troy had to stop and fill his lungs again as the fear of rejection slid through his veins and chilled his blood despite the warm cocoon they lay in.

Silas slid his leg between Troy's thigh and squeezed him tighter, the steady cadence of his heart beating against Troy's back.

"My science t-teacher…I crushed on him. Hard. And he noticed. Rather than drawing lines between us like he should have done with a starstruck kid, he encouraged my blatant flirting." Cold sweat beaded on Troy's forehead.

Silas didn't shift, his steady exhales bathing the top of Troy's head with warmth and giving him the courage to continue.

"We exchanged numbers, and through the rest of

third quarter, we texted. Sent p-pictures of…you know." Troy expelled a shaky breath. "He told me he loved me, couldn't wait until I turned eighteen in May…I'm sure you get the idea."

His stomach churned as he pushed against his memory's flashing images. The handsome smile that had first captured his attention. Laughing eyes full of warmth and teasing. Murmured words meant to entice.

At one time, they had all filled his heart with flutters, but he'd learned the hard way how a man's arrogance led to deception.

"What happened, angel?" Silas's voice soothed rather than demanded he continue.

Troy inhaled until it hurt before speaking the rest. The shit that had come after the buildup of what he'd thought had been a beautiful thing.

"The night I turned eighteen, I snuck out of my parent's house and went to his apartment. I was more than willing and ready to have my fantasies fulfilled, my virginity given up to the man who claimed to love me more than life."

A sense of choking tightened his throat, and Troy opened his eyes, blinking into focus the bureau against the wall. He reminding himself of where he was, his reality in that moment, to keep from reliving that terrifying night. His teacher couldn't touch him, wasn't there in the bedroom with him and Silas.

"He got rough," Troy whispered, wishing for numbness rather than the rawness bleeding through his voice. "Held me down—freaked me the fuck out." Troy blew out a tension-ridden exhale, wishing he could rid his mind as easily.

"You changed your mind."

Troy nodded at Silas's murmur.

"Yes." He swallowed audibly, but the sense of helplessness still haunted him, still twisted his stomach. "but he didn't stop."

Silas cursed, his body going rigid. "Goddamn red flag," he muttered, but before Troy could react, he continued. "That's why you needed to hear my voice that first time I fucked you, isn't it? You needed to know it was me—not him."

Trembling and unable to speak, Troy nodded.

"Tell me the rest," Silas demanded, his tone hard —but his touch remained soft as he rubbed Troy's arm, raising goosebumps along his skin.

Troy took a few seconds to steel himself for rejection but couldn't stop the adrenaline causing him to shake regardless of his stiffened muscles. "A-afterward..." He inhaled until it hurt, trying to get a better hold on himself. "Afterward, he told me I'd asked for it. Told me to quit crying like a baby. I-I spent a week walking around in shame made even worse by the fact he ignored me in class or when I saw him in the h-hallways. He didn't return my texts. I didn't eat, couldn't sleep." A desire to curl up in a ball and withdraw from Silas swept through him, but he needed to finish. Deal with the consequences of sharing his story.

"It was my parents threatening to take me to a shrink that made me break down and explain what had happened." Tears leaked from Troy's eyes at the memory of their love, their support—but also out of fear that Silas wouldn't react in the same. "They wanted to press charges, and it was another week before I agreed. We went to court facing a jury made up of middle-aged adults, mostly male when we'd hoped for empathetic mothers."

Recalling their looks of judgment roused anger inside Troy, quelling some of his anxiety that weakened his legs.

"The exchanged texts, a lot of which included me begging for my teacher to give me what I wanted and be my first, swayed them during deliberation. It didn't help that I was an out and proud gay kid who flirted with everybody even though I'd saved myself for that special someone. If I'd been a girl, the outcome would have been different."

He attempted to keep his tone light to portray a stronger character, but long-term depression and anger leaked through his words.

"The asshole got away with rape, only losing his job when he should have been put behind bars. His complete lack of integrity, his dishonesty on the stand is what led me to study law. It's the event that made me who I am. Yes, I'd led him on, yes, I'd asked for it countless times, but…"

A vise squeezed Troy's chest, and he bit his lip. He waited, his heart ready to fracture.

Silas shifted, and Troy clenched his eyes shut, sure his lover wanted distance between them. Strong hands rolled Troy onto his back rather than pushing him away.

"Look at me."

Breath held, Troy did as told, finding intense hazel eyes peering at him from where Silas propped on his elbow over him.

"You have nothing to be ashamed of. You said no. End of. Gay, straight, male, female…no means no regardless of how far things went between the two of you. He's more than an asshole." Silas went tight-lipped for a second, his jaw clenching. "And he deserves to rot in hell for what he did to you."

Wetness welled in Troy's eyes, and a shudder rippled over him.

Silas studied him, swiping the tears that escaped with his thumbs. "You thought your past would change how I feel about you."

Troy gulped and nodded even though Silas hadn't asked a question.

A soft smile lightened the intensity in Silas's eyes, causing some of the tension to leak from Troy's body. "Silly boy. Don't you know you've burrowed deep inside me?"

The release of anxiety and fear over Silas's possible reaction swept through him like a spring rainstorm—and he couldn't help the snicker rising from his relief and the filthy route his brain went at Silas's words.

Silas's gaze narrowed. "Should I even ask?"

"Would you ever…" Troy bit his lower lip, drawing Silas's focus to his mouth. The sudden giddiness and the desire to love on Silas Barlowe took his mind a different route from the heaviness from seconds before.

"Let you top me?" Silas finished the trailed off sentence lingering between them.

Troy's heart thumped in his chest as he stared up at the sexiest man to walk the earth. Rumpled dark hair, the blackest lashes around gorgeous hazel eyes. The strong nose and chin, luscious mouth slowly curling up at the corners.

His face answered for him.

"You curious kitty," Troy breathed past his widening grin. "You would, wouldn't you?"

"Yes." Silas's eyes went serious, his smile fading. "But only because I can trust you to stop if I say no."

Goddamn him.

Tears once more rolled, and Silas tugged Troy tight, holding him until emotional exhaustion took him under.

Silas

Silas untangled his body from the slight one sprawled over him in his bed. His elfin angel was a goddamn octopus when sleeping.

And Silas fucking loved it.

But he'd spent the better part of the weekend planning how to best focus that rage he'd tucked away, and knowing Chávez woke with the sun, Silas forced himself to set his lover aside for a brief time.

He padded silently across his penthouse suite, closing himself into his office. Streaks of sun licked at the backs of Boston's skyline, washing the city with golden light. A new morning, a new beginning.

The same he wanted to give to his boy.

Silas put through the call he'd been thinking about since Troy had opened up about his past and allowed Silas inside his head. "I want everything you can find on the man," he told Chávez seconds into their conversation. "The first time he jacked off, the last time he took a shit."

Chávez didn't argue with Silas's demand. The man knew Silas would pay—and well.

"Find what he values the most so I can destroy it. Destroy *him*." Silas's tone had never escaped with such stark determination, but he couldn't help the emotions holding him on edge.

"Do I want to know why you sound ready to knife this guy to death?" Chávez asked, his tone as serious as Silas's.

"It's personal," Silas bit out the words, fighting to keep a red haze of irrational behavior under control since the call had riled it back up.

Finding out the truth of that red flag on top of the drive-by shooting that could have ripped Troy from Silas forever had taken him to an edge he only experienced with his sister.

Love.

The word rang in his ears, and Silas didn't deny the intense feelings he had for the beautiful man he held almost every night since he'd sauntered into Silas's life.

The morning after Troy had shared his vulnerabilities, Silas hadn't woken Troy up before the sun with a dick in his ass. He'd kissed him. Cuddled and worshiped every inch of his skin, including the leaking dick packed away in blue silk.

Fucking panties did Silas in every time.

He'd swallowed down Troy's spurting cum while painting the sheets with his own from merely grinding against the mattress and listening to his sexy boy's whimpers and moans.

Troy Emerson was the hottest fucking human on the planet. He belonged to Silas—and Silas took care of what was his.

"I want it all, Chavéz," he repeated his demand, pushing aside the arousing memory from two days before. "Then we're going to find a way to take his ass down."

"You got it," Chávez didn't hesitate to reply. "I'll be in touch."

"Oh… has Noah Madden contacted you yet? I gave him your credentials and number to help out in the case the assistant DA is building against me."

"He called Friday afternoon, and yes, I agreed to take the job."

"I don't care how you get the shit we need. Just find it. Dig deeper than you ever have—I'll make it worth your while."

"You always do, Silas."

Already breathing easier, Silas hung up and sat back in his home office chair, his stare on the sticky note clinging to his desk naming the man who'd prompted his call.

Redmond Lennon no longer had a life.

He just didn't know it yet.

14

Troy

A week passed with no arrest and no leads in the shooting that had changed Troy's life—all for the best.

He had shared his past, the reason behind his triggers, and Silas had only held him tighter, believed his every word, trusted him...enough to agree to allow Troy full access to his body.

Not that Troy was in a rush to top. The idea scared him as much as bottoming first had. What if he wasn't any good at it? What if he shot his load the second he breached Silas's ass?

Just the thought turned him rock hard, his erection unflagging even at the idea of failure.

Maybe someday, but Troy could wait. He longed more to further prove himself to Silas who had weaseled his way inside Troy's head and had laid waste to his determination to stay focused.

The pre-trial loomed closer, and he was anxious to sit by Noah and face the group of potential jurors. He would help create a jury of Silas's peers, people who understood their lives being threatened and the instinctual need to survive.

So far, the only discovery lay in circumstance. There was no real evidence that Silas's defense team was aware that would create a slam dunk case for the murder charges their client faced.

Troy had high hopes, clinging to the idea of *more* once Silas was cleared and set free to live his life. He didn't doubt his own feelings, and after sharing all his secrets and not being turned away, he felt sure of Silas's as well.

The morning of the pre-trial found Troy in Silas's bed as usual—beneath him, knees near his ears, ass stuffed full with a spent dick. Both panted, Silas's face nuzzling in Troy's neck.

"We gotta go."

"Yeah," Troy agreed, breathless, but couldn't shift the weight from atop him—didn't *want* to move.

Groaning, Silas pushed up to a plank, and gaze locked with Troy, slowly dragged his cock from Troy's ass.

Words swelled inside Troy, but he bit his lip, refusing to be the first to say it like he'd done with his teacher.

Silas smirked and bent his head low enough that his breath washed over Troy's lips. "Yeah."

Troy blinked and stared as Silas left him alone, intent on the bathroom. Surely—

"You'd better shower in the other bathroom, otherwise, we're never going to get out of here on time."

Troy sank into Silas's bed, releasing a heavy exhale which did nothing to settle the giddiness inside his chest. Had Silas read his mind? Had that single word he'd murmured been an agreement from the emotions that no doubt filled Troy's eyes while he'd gazed up at him?

"Hurry up, boy!"

Grinning, Troy rolled over and to his feet. Fifteen minutes, he noted on the alarm clock, until they needed to be on the road for the courthouse.

He nicked his chin while hastily dragging a razor over his chin but managed to stop the bleeding with a piece of tissue. Even though he was prettier than Silas and needed more time for his beautification process that Silas joked about, he stood ready by the door, waiting on his lover.

"Have you seen my cell?" Silas hollered from the bedroom.

"No," Troy called back.

"Can you check my office?"

Troy headed toward the penthouse's other room that overlooked Boston. Silas's cell sat atop his desk along with a few folders and haphazardly strewn papers.

The bottom half of a yellow sticky note beneath one folder caught his eye.

Lennon.

Frowning, Troy slowly pushed the covering away, revealing the sticky note in its entirety.

Raymond Lennon.

Alarm raised the hairs on Troy's neck. He righted the folder and picked up Silas's cell, his chest constricted and forehead deeply grooved. Why had Silas written down the name of his rapist?

With how protective Silas was, he shouldn't have been surprised, but what possible reason could he have to do such a thing?

Troy handed over Silas's cell before exiting the condo, his lips pressed tight, not ready to open a can of possible worms considering what they faced that morning.

His heartbeat throbbed in his ears, slight dizziness lighting his head until he sat in Silas's car. Why, he couldn't help but wonder. The truth of Silas's nature, his possessiveness, created all kinds of scenarios in Troy's head, made him question his lover's intent.

They faced jury selection, and Troy needed to be at the top of his game. Troubling thoughts and apprehension would mess with his head and his ability to help Noah.

"Why did you write down his name?" Troy blurted as Silas sped them toward the courthouse.

"What?" Silas glanced in his side mirror to change lanes.

Troy's heart raced along with the Mercedes's engine. "Redmond Lennon—you wrote down his name on a sticky note. I saw it on your desk."

"Oh." A rare moment of hesitation on Silas's part pinged something inside Troy's chest. "It's nothing," Silas stated without glancing over at him. "I just wondered what had happened to the fucker who hurt my man."

While that last bit should have made Troy's insides swoon, the way in which it had been delivered felt like manipulation.

Deviousness.

A lie.

Jaw clenching against the sudden churning of his stomach, Troy turned his focus out the passenger window. Boston's downtown and cars surged past, but he couldn't focus beyond the thoughts of sure trickery in his head.

What else had Silas lied about? What truths had he kept from Troy? Was every word, every touch, a form of deceit?

Or was Troy overthinking in his usual attempts to protect his heart?

Silas took his hand, threading their fingers together—Troy responding on autopilot even though he wanted to hold back.

"Thank you."

"For?" Troy asked, still not giving Silas his eyes.

"Everything—all your hours spent in helping Noah. Me. My sister."

Did Silas truly mean the words that sounded sincere, or was it a pretense to cover whatever it was he hid from Troy?

Too many damn questions roused to life inside Troy, but he didn't have the energy or extra brain cells to spare.

It wasn't the time for a confrontation that would leave Troy even more wrecked than he was. Shoving against his suspicions, he focused on the task ahead of him, proving that he could do his job without interference or compromise.

He had a jury to help pick, and even if he found out Silas had lied to him, ruining what they had, he wanted the verdict to go in Silas's favor.

15

Silas

The lie hadn't slid as easily from Silas's tongue as others had in the past. Keeping the truth from Troy didn't sit right in his gut, but if Troy knew what he had planned and put into motion, he would be pissed. Troy's integrity would demand Silas end what he'd started to bury the rapist who deserved to have the skin sliced from his body until he bled out.

And Silas wouldn't agree to Troy's wants. Couldn't. His protective instincts were animalistic in nature, uncontrolled by thought processes and self-awareness. He would hurt anyone who threatened those he loved.

He wouldn't hesitate if faced with needing to do so again. If Troy knew the darker side of Silas's character, he would run for the hills as any sane person would.

Being honest in what he planned would end what he and Troy had going, and he liked what they shared. Loved it to the point he would defend it with his life if need be.

Troy held his hand as they drove to the courthouse, allowed the tether of affection between them even though unease radiated off his slender shoulders.

Silas's boy had every intention of being in Noah's position someday, staring down people in the witness stand, but did he recognize the fact his strength lay in the work behind the scenes?

Noah had sung his praises, doing nothing to hinder Silas's interest in his employee even though he helped with Silas's case. While not outright permission to make Troy his, Silas had taken Noah's words for what they were—a stamp of approval.

He had to release his hold on Troy to park. Couldn't rub his thumb over Troy's hand as they hurried up the stairs past reporters wanting Silas's thoughts on what awaited him inside.

Rich, hardly famous, but still a man of interest to the public intent on any hint of a juicy story. He would much rather drag Troy into his arms and kiss him senseless while shutters and cell phones clicked to out him, but he refrained.

For now, he again promised himself, anxious for the shit of the charges to disappear in the rearview mirror of his life.

Awareness of Troy beside him, the scent of his goddamn bodywash on the smooth skin hidden beneath a navy suit, kept Silas's focus off the drone of words between the lawyers, the judge, and the potential jurors answering questions.

He trusted Noah and Troy to do their best in creating a jury that would favor his story over the gathered circumstantial evidence.

Silas hinged his hope on them.

And at the end of the long-as-fuck day in the hard, wooden chair beneath his ass, assurance they'd done their jobs rested in Noah's eyes. If only Silas felt the same. He still couldn't help but fear the small chance that bars would replace the young man he wanted as his ball and chain.

Troy wouldn't look at Silas as they readied to leave but busied himself gathering up the files and papers on the table in front of them. Even though Silas could feel the heat of his lover, draw the strawberry scent of his lip gloss deep into his lungs, he could sense the wall between them.

One created by his lie.

He needed to be honest in all things—but how without it tearing them apart?

The three men went out for an early dinner, seated in a dark corner at Noah's request in an upscale Italian restaurant in the North End. Noah sat across from Silas, Troy on his right. His boy still wouldn't give him his eyes, finding his linen napkin, glass of red wine, and the plate of pasta in front of him more important than Silas.

Silas's stomach churned, and he hardly touched his food.

Their discussion centered on the upcoming trial, the men and women on the jury, and what possible angles the assistant DA might steer toward in his hopes to sway them toward a guilty verdict.

Rather than demand Troy look at him, Silas suffered in silence, not wanting to embarrass his young lover. And being needy, showing his weakness in front of others, wasn't something Silas Barlowe did.

Noah offered a bit of coaching for when Silas took the stand, but Silas knew he wouldn't deviate from the story he'd given Detective Marsh from the very beginning. Nothing the prosecution team brought against him would change his retelling of the events that had ended up with him covered in blood and Brian Parsons as dead as a fucking doorknob. He would stick to the truth as he saw it, knowing the collateral damage that would await him on the other end.

It would hurt like fuck, but he would have Troy to ease his heartache until Grace forgave him.

At least, he hoped to still have the elfin waif in his arms. With how Troy ignored him, Silas began to truly fear he'd fucked up in a way that might not be fixable.

Silas and Troy stood beside each other on the sidewalk as they got ready to leave the restaurant, only inches separating them, but it felt like a goddamn mile.

Noah waved and drove off, leaving them alone.

"Will you come over tonight?" Silas asked quietly rather than assuming Troy would spend the night in his bed.

"No." Troy snipped the single worded reply, lips quickly pressing tight once more

Silas's stomach bottomed out. At least Troy hadn't made up lies as an excuse like he would have done in the kid's situation.

Silas stuffed down his disappointment in Troy's answer—and himself. They'd driven together, but their return to Silas's building where Troy's car waited remained silent.

Tense, and for the first time, not of the sexual sort.

Pain lanced through Silas's chest, and he knew that a few simple words would crack the ice, but he feared, *fuck*, how he feared the consequences of his choice to stick with his lie.

Stomach in a hard knot, Silas parked and turned off the engine.

Troy climbed from the car without a word and started toward his own, leaving Silas gripping his steering wheel and cursing.

He couldn't go another hour like that. Wouldn't.

Fucking *couldn't* without losing his goddamn mind.

Shoving open the door, he called out to Troy and hurried after him. "Troy!" he called again when the man didn't stop.

Troy stood by his driver door but didn't reach for the handle. He also didn't turn.

Inhaling until it hurt, Silas strode across his parking garage, mind racing over how to make things right.

Car wheels squeaked while tightly turning the corner beside him, but it was the sudden roar of the engine from a lead foot that sent Silas rushing forward. He leaped, and the oncoming sedan smashed into the passenger's back fender of Troy's car. The force of the impact shoved Troy's vehicle into the car parked alongside, sending the two men it hit tumbling toward the ground.

Air ripped from Silas's lungs from the impact of his body slamming into the neighboring vehicle, but at least they hadn't been pinned between metal.

Troy...

Tires squealed, taking the roaring engine and the fucker who'd tried to run Silas down from the garage.

Silas once more pushed himself off Troy, his eyes flitting over the younger man's face, hands frantic to make sure he hadn't been hurt.

"Fuck." Troy groaned, wincing as Silas slid a hand over his shoulder.

"Are you okay, angel? Fuck…tell me you're okay."

"I'm fine." Troy grimaced and sat up in the tiny space between the two cars. "Being with you isn't good for my health."

A sense of helplessness washed over Silas, and he pulled Troy in tight against his chest. He bit back a sob as Troy melted against his chest rather than pushing away.

Two attempts on his life had put his lover in danger, which roused his murderous rage.

Again.

He didn't doubt the dark vehicle without a front plate was the same one that had carried the shooter. And while he didn't have time to check out the driver, he knew beyond a shadow of a doubt he was the man who'd held the Glock.

"You're staying with me tonight," Silas stated, his tone refusing any answer but agreement.

Thank fuck Troy didn't feel the need to argue because Silas had shit that needed said.

Only the truth would break down the wall his lies had erected between them.

16

Troy

Troy was quiet while he and Silas peeled off their suits later that night. They'd once again spent hours with law enforcement over the attempt made on Silas's life. There was no other explanation for what had happened.

A drive-by and near-intentional running down with a car indicated both had been aimed—literally—at Silas.

Rage and fear mixed in a sickening brew inside Troy's stomach long after the event.

Silas's first reaction had been to look after him. Check him for injury, same as when they'd been shot at.

The man was beyond possessive, instinctively so.

How far would he go to protect those he loved? They hadn't shared the words, but Troy knew the look in Silas's eyes whenever he caught the man staring at him.

But Silas wouldn't meet Troy's gaze as they stripped and stepped into the shower together.

Silence reigned between them as it had most of the day, but he allowed Silas his usual tender care, soap-slickened hands running over every inch of his skin. Troy's dick hardened regardless of his suspicions of lying and manipulation, but Silas kept his touch clinical as though sensitive toward Troy's unease.

"If I hid something from you…" Silas finally broke the tense quiet between them while kneeling before him and washing his calves.

Troy waited for him to continue, his breaths going shallow as Silas stood and finally met his gaze head-on. Fear poured from hazel eyes usually closed off to all but lust and longing, causing Troy's stomach to tighten.

"I've never allowed myself to rely on anyone but Grace," Silas finally stated quietly above the sounds of the showerheads pelting their skin. He studied Troy's face as though memorizing every line. "Never thought I could, but you've proven yourself time and again these past couple of weeks."

Warmth spread through Troy's limbs regardless of his need to protect himself.

"I—I don't want to lose what we've found, Troy." Silas swallowed hard and pulled his focus off Troy's face, clearly struggling with being on unsteady ground. "I'm so damn afraid that you'll hate who I am at the most instinctive part of me. The things I would do in order to protect those I l—"

Troy pressed his fingertips to Silas's mouth, silencing him as tenderness swelled inside his heart regardless of his own unease and suspicions. He wanted the man trembling before him—desperately. Longed to hold onto him, assure him that what grew between them was as telling and as real as fingerprints were evidence.

"Wait until you're cleared and we have a future ahead of us before talking about this," Troy murmured, water dripping from his lips and eyelashes.

Silas's eyelids closed, and he swallowed audibly. "What if we don't have a future?"

The cocky, assured man hadn't ever shown such vulnerability, and it sent an ache of empathy through Troy's chest.

"I'm fighting for one," Troy whispered even though questions and truth still lay unspoken between them. "Will you?"

Silas wrapped his strong arms around Troy and clutched him close, his face pressed against Troy's throat. But he didn't speak.

Allowing Silas his privacy, Troy held him tight as though he was the rock for the bigger man.

Suspicions of what Silas had done lay heavy in

Troy's mind, and not voicing them, not demanding complete honesty, questioned the integrity he'd clung to for years. Knowing the things in Silas's mind, he feared, would tear him apart.

People tended to look out for number one as he'd learned the hard way.

Misplaced loyalty had brought Troy to his knees, almost ruined his life, and he struggled with setting aside that trauma.

Was Silas hanging onto him because of who Troy worked for? Did he think to sway the investigations to keep the prosecution from getting the guilty verdict they hoped for?

The way Silas clung to him, the fingertips grasping at his back, the slight shivers rippling over his hard body…

Troy expelled a heavy breath, closed his eyes, and prayed like hell the emotional connection, the blooming love he felt was real and would be enough to see them through to the end.

Three days before the trial, Troy sat across from Silas eating breakfast they'd cooked together. Quietness hung over the table, both seemingly lost in their heads over the near future.

He and Noah had gone over every possible scenario of Silas's upcoming time in the witness stand, asking him questions the assistant DA might throw out in attempts to catch him off guard or to twist prior words.

Silas had said he was ready and appeared confident.

But uncertainty lingered in the back of Troy's mind regardless of their strengthening relationship.

The nasty fender-bender of Troy's car had brought them closer together. The insurance aspect, however, had been a headache that had made Troy bitchy since the morning before. With no possible way to identify the asshole who'd smashed into his car, the deductible fell onto Troy, and while he had the five hundred he would have to put toward the damage, he didn't feel he should have to—

Troy's cell rang, breaking into his thoughts, and he grinned at his best friend's name on the screen.

"You're alive!" he answered with a laugh, the first to fall from his lips in weeks.

Chase didn't joke back but blurted out, "Did you see the news?" His guarded tone caused Troy's smile to fade.

Silas caught his gaze, his brow furrowing.

"No." Troy stared at Silas while answering Chase, adrenaline rushing through him.

"Lennon's dead," Chase said.

Lennon. Dead.

The reality of Chase's statement took a few seconds for Troy to process. The blood drained from his face as he stared unseeing across the table. "What?" he heard himself ask as though his brain needed clarity.

"Raymond Lennon," Chase repeated. "His wife found him hanging from their garage rafters yesterday morning."

He imagined Raymond's handsome face swollen and discolored.

Nausea stirred in his stomach, his coffee threatening to come up.

"The fuck?" Troy whispered, blinking the image of Raymond's dangling body from his mind. Silas came back into focus, his stare intense.

"What's wrong?" Silas mouthed, but Chase continued, demanding Troy's attention.

"He faced financial ruin—he left a suicide note."

Troy rubbed a hand down over his face and closed his eyes, remembering the sticky note on Silas's desk. Recalling Silas's words in the shower when he'd seemed ready to uncover all his sins…

"I—I have to go," Troy whispered and swallowed hard to keep the contents of his stomach in place.

"Troy—"

"I'll call later, Chase. Promise." Troy hit end and stood up from the table on shaking legs.

Silas's cell also rang, and he glanced at the screen.

Troy noted Chávez, the private investigator who'd been helping with their case flashing on the screen before Silas silenced the call.

"What's wrong?" Silas repeated, flipping his phone facedown on the table.

"My rapist is dead," Troy answered, a question in his tone—and in his damn mind.

Silas's face didn't flinch, but a flicker of satisfaction lit his hardened eyes for a brief second.

Too fucking telling.

The death hadn't come as a surprise.

Heat flushed through Troy's body, and not the delicious kind that ended with the two of them fucking.

Silas had feared Troy learning who he was at the core—but Troy had already figured the man out. That box Troy had originally put Silas Barlowe into? He definitely deserved to stay the fuck there.

Troy's stomach contents relaxed, but he clenched his jaw. Without another word, he got up and moved toward the bedroom, his muscles quivering and pulse pounding.

"Troy, hold on!"

Like hell he would. He'd stopped Silas from speaking, thinking the truth could wait. How wrong he'd been. Lennon's death felt too much like premeditated deception. Worse than any lie tossed out in the heat of confrontation or unease.

Troy yanked on a hoodie he'd left on the top of the bureau the night before.

"Troy."

Ignoring Silas in the bedroom doorway, Troy

shoved on his sneakers without socks. His insides quaked as his heart shattered.

"What are you doing?" Alarm, a hint of fear laced Silas's tone.

"Leaving," he rasped.

"Why? What is going on, Troy?" The man sounded desperate, but Troy hardened his resolve.

He straightened and met Silas's stare head-on even though he wanted to break down and sob. A good ten feet separated the men, but the tension of unspoken words, mistrust, and betrayal lay thick between them.

While there was no way Silas had been physically involved in that asshole's hanging—they'd been together most of the weekend—Troy didn't trust his lack of involvement.

"Did you do it?" Troy asked.

No hint of emotion showed on Silas's face. "I had no hand in killing that man."

Troy studied him, couldn't read shit on his expressionless face—but Silas's word choice was telling as fuck. "What did you do, Silas? And don't bullshit me right now. Tell me the fucking truth— about every goddamn thing—or I'll walk out that damn door and never come back."

Their gazes clashed, the tension rising to the point Troy struggled to inhale.

"Silas…" Fuck, he didn't want to beg, but he couldn't help himself. He knew his eyes pleaded, but the hurt, the agony ripping at his chest was too much to bear.

"I didn't kill him."

Feeling as though the ground swayed beneath his feet, Troy tore his focus off Silas and grabbed his wallet off the bureau.

Silas wouldn't budge from the doorway when he approached. "You don't believe me."

"Get out of my way, Silas," Troy barely managed to whisper past the tightness in his throat.

Troy lifted his gaze off Silas's bare chest for steady, hazel eyes. No hint of guilt lay in his orbs, simply a resolved coldness Troy had seen dozens of times.

Silas lied.

While he might not have had a *hand* in physically taking Lennon's life, he was without doubt responsible for the man's demise.

A half-lie was still a lie. Period.

"Please." Silas stood like a pillar in front of Troy, keeping him from leaving, as if he could prohibit Troy from making his own choice.

Troy knew the one word he trusted Silas would honor.

"No."

Pain rose in Silas's eyes, his shoulders sagging as though defeated. He let out a shuddered exhale and stepped to the side.

Legs trembling, Troy slipped around him, antsy as hell to put distance between them even though his arms longed to reach out and hold on until the storm passed.

"Troy, please," Silas begged, but Troy moved silently across the kitchen, past their half-emptied plates, and grabbed his keys off the counter. They clanked together in his shaking hand.

"We'll talk after the trial, Silas," he choked out without looking behind him. "I need time to deal with this shit."

"Troy—"

The door snicked shut behind Troy, and he leaned against it, heart pounding and eyes stinging.

There wouldn't be a single shred of concrete evidence to link Silas to Raymond's death—same as there hadn't been enough uncovered to prove him guilty of murdering Brian Parsons.

Troy stumbled toward the elevator, his thoughts a riotous mess.

He didn't care about Lennon's death—took a little bit of satisfaction in knowing he no longer drew breath past his lying tongue, if he was being honest with himself.

His integrity demanded he learn the truth of both situations, but the feelings that had strengthened for Silas since their first meeting made him wish he could just ignore his lover's involvement.

His lies and manipulation.

Even the outright deceit that curdled Troy's stomach.

He wanted to believe Silas, longed for it to the point tears slid down his cheeks when he climbed in the back of a cab.

But no matter the miles growing between him and Silas, the war inside didn't sway toward one side or the other.

He recalled the way Silas had reacted after the attempts on his life. He'd only been concerned for Troy. The memory of fear in his eyes, the frantic hands searching over Troy's body in desperation to make sure he hadn't been injured…

Silas loved him to the point nothing else mattered—including his own virtue. The man was loyal to a fault.

"Fuck," Troy whispered and swallowed hard. Head tipped back against the cab's seat, he heaved a heavy exhale.

Three days until trial.

Three days to get his head set straight on whether he was willing to overlook those sins or forgive in the name of love.

17

Silas

Silas sat unmoving, staring straight ahead as though unaffected by the prosecution's opening statements.

But it was awareness of the man seated beside him, the scent of strawberries and vanilla bodywash filling his lungs that knotted his insides tight with pain.

Troy hadn't returned his calls or texts since the morning after that Lennon fucker's wife had found him dangling from a rope around his neck. While Silas hadn't lied about physical involvement, he'd definitely played a part in the man's suicide.

It had been a few carefully placed words in influential men's ears and one favor called in to a man who Silas had shit on that had led to the rapist's financial ruin he'd mentioned in his suicide note.

Silas's heart lay heavy in his chest as he put on a

confident face for those in the courtroom. Rarely did shame over his actions eat at him, but for once he wondered if he'd gone too far. Would his instinctive need to protect land him behind emotional bars? Would he end up imprisoned by his own nature? He hated admitting guilt, let alone defeat.

Somehow, he would find a way to prove himself to Troy, to get him understand his drive to watch over those he considered his. Surely he could be made to see that love, loyalty, and family came first above all things—even doing what was right in the eyes of man.

He could feel Grace's presence behind him, the quiet support she offered.

Silas had every confidence she would eventually forgive his actions that being on the stand would uncover, but he feared never getting the chance to make things right. He knew what Noah had up his sleeve to discredit some of the evidence and witnesses, but would it be enough? Would the jury staring at him with judgment already in their eyes be swayed to believe his story about that morning Brian Parsons showed up at Grace's house?

How could they if Troy, a man he loved desperately, couldn't? His lover hadn't even given him a chance to state his case.

Detective Asshole Marsh was called to the stand, pulling Silas's focus back to the trial of his life.

After being sworn in and his credentials bragged

about to the jury, the detective settled in with a cocky tilt to his head, his gaze hard on Silas with a goddamn glint, like he carried the key to Silas's conviction.

Greg Harlan stood before him, hands clasped behind his back, and drew the asshole's focus off Silas by stating, "Would you please walk us through your findings on the morning of Brian Parsons's murder."

"Objection," Noah called out without rolling his eyes like Silas expected he wanted to do. "Leading the witness."

"Sustained," the judge stated firmly, his face a mask of indifference. "Please rephrase your question, Mr. Harlan."

"Please tell us about your response and what you found after being dispatched for the 911 call placed by Silas Barlowe."

Detective Marsh started in with a professional, no bullshit tone, stating facts as he'd noted them from the time he'd driven up to Grace's house, lights flashing and sirens blaring, to the handcuffing of Silas for his ride to the station for questioning.

Silas had been covered in blood, and a dead body lay on the floor of Grace Barlowe's kitchen.

"It was Mr. Barlowe's lack of remorse for stabbing a man to death that appeared suspicious—"

"Objection," Noah interrupted at the same time

Silas cursed in his head. "The witness can't speak to the defendant's motive or feelings."

"Sustained."

Silas attempted to relax his insides, but tension twisted him tight. His attention pulled in two directions—to the man on the witness chair and the one beside him that his body couldn't ignore.

"Detective, in your opinion, how did Mr. Barlowe appear to react to Brian Parsons's death?" Greg encouraged him to continue.

"Mr. Barlowe was very matter of fact. Calm. Seemingly unaffected by the events that had transpired."

"Is that usual in your experience?" Greg asked.

"No," Detective Marsh stated firmly. "Usually they're upset, going into shock, on the verge of panic. I've never seen someone who took another life remain unmoved."

The asshole went on trying to smear Silas's name, repeating what had been said about him in social media and various news outlets about his ruthless business practices—and Noah objected once more over his lack of physical evidence as it pertained to the case at hand.

Any good businessman worth the shirt on their back tended toward ruthlessness, Silas wanted to spew. A man needed to be cold and calculating to make it in a cutthroat world. He'd learned from the best and lived the high life in proof of that truth.

The detective painted a grim picture of Silas, but it wasn't anything new, nothing recently uncovered to convince the jury he had a deeper, darker nature. All attempts to make him look like a big, bad villain fell on deaf ears to those who kept up on social media or followed news about local charities.

And just because Silas Barlow was a shark when it came to legally making money didn't mean he'd killed a man who'd attacked him in order to prove his superiority.

Silas sat and stared the detective down, his features relaxed, gaze unfazed by the bullshit spewing from the man's lips.

Detective Marsh brought up their lone shitty discovery that could rouse suspicion, but Silas reminded himself it was nothing but circumstantial.

The security cameras at Grace's home had been shut down the morning of Brian Parsons's death.

Suspicious, but hardly damning.

Worse though was the fact that the man who had installed the system was the only one able to control it.

Silas Barlow.

There was no physical evidence to prove he'd killed Mr. Parsons in a fit of rage like the prosecution team had hoped for. How they'd even gotten that far into trial on circumstantial evidence baffled Silas's mind, but enough inferred possible intentions.

It would be up to the jury to decide—Silas just hoped they remembered the *law* when debating the verdict.

Once Detective Marsh finished spewing nothing but his suspicions and the bit of truth regarding how he had found things at Grace's house, Greg finished with the asshole.

"Does the defense have any questions for this witness?" the judge asked.

"Yes, Your Honor." Noah studied a paper in front of him as though unhurried, perhaps too busy for such trivial bullshit. The second the judge opened his mouth to prompt him, Noah stood, smoothing down his tie.

Silas knew what he planned—had learned a mere hour prior to trial. He fought to keep his glee from showing on his face.

Noah approached the jury and turned to face the detective for his cross-examination. His intentional action gave those who held Silas's future in their hands a direct view of the asshole's face—his eyes.

"Detective Marsh, would you be so kind as to inform the jury of your connection with Jose Garcia?"

The detective blinked. Paled. Cleared his throat. "Who?"

Silas bit back a snicker, *finally* a sense of his usual confidence swelling inside him. He wanted to reach over and grab Troy's hand, tug his lover closer, and proclaim his innocent intentions.

"Jose Garcia." Noah didn't shift or remove his focus from the man on the witness stand. "The drug runner—your informer. The one you were caught accepting a payoff from in order to keep silent about his dealings."

Detective Marsh swallowed audibly, and Silas shot his focus over to the assistant DA. He sat unmoving, lips in a thin line.

"Still don't remember his name?" Noah walked across the hardwood floor, the heel of his left shoe squeaking in the silence.

Troy handed him a file, which Noah took to the judge's bench.

"Let the court reflect I am entering documenta-tion that we received early this morning in regards to Detective Marsh's professional ethics as relevant to this case."

Silas wanted to laugh in the asshole detective's face who suddenly wasn't acting so damn tough.

Noah also handed a copy of the evidence to Greg who quickly glanced down to rifle through the papers as Noah continued.

"Your Honor, would you be so kind as to share with the court the findings on page three?" Noah asked.

"Detective Marsh was caught twice in under-handed business dealings with Jose Garcia—on camera, on wiretap. The man in charge of the internal investigations was his close friend. As noted on page two, there was an exchange of funds from Detective Marsh to that same internal affairs officer on the day the investigation began."

The detective didn't slouch, didn't visibly flinch, but guilt etched on his paling face.

Greg Harlan's cheeks reddened, a muscle twitching in his jaw as jurors shifted in their chairs.

Silas fought to keep his expression placid.

A few minutes after Noah tore Detective Marsh's character to dust, the assistant DA muttered his refusal to further question his witness.

18

Troy

Even though over twelve inches separated Troy from Silas, he could feel the man's heat, the draw from his body like a magnet to metal. He wanted to brush his leg against Silas's, show him physical support, but the fact they sat in a court of law proved more a deterrent than Troy's continued hurt and anger.

Silas remained unmoved, as though unaffected by the witnesses and their speculations. His cool gaze and his continued lack of remorse, as stated by Noah, was not evidence enough to prove he'd done more than protect himself from Brian Parsons.

But...

Troy had gotten to know Silas on a deeper level than most. Silas had let down his walls, allowed Troy to see past what he showed the world, his vulnerabilities when it came to those in his inner circle. Those he cared about—Troy included.

Heart-aching desire rose inside Troy over the lack of contact the previous three days…but he reminded himself of the devious answers concerning Silas's involvement in his rapist's death.

Had Silas lied to the detective as well? To Noah?

He'd kept the real truth from Grace concerning her security system being shut off that morning, and the explanation that would come out once Silas took the stand could prove destructive.

Traumatic enough to cause a wedge between Silas and his sister.

And if the fallout left Silas without the support of Grace…

Troy fought off the need to swallow hard at the thought. He wanted to be the one beside Silas, he wished—regardless of Silas's lies and withholding of the full truth—to be the man by his side. He hoped to offer comfort if Silas's sister held a grudge over something he'd done out of love.

Fingernails digging into his palms to keep from scrubbing a hand down over his face, Troy sat still as the prosecution called Dr. Loveling, the medical examiner, to the stand. In a stiff black suit built more for a man's body than a stately woman's, Dr. Loveling swore over a Bible. Her hair pulled back in a severe bun, more gray than brown, stretching out the crow's feet at the corners of her eyes.

Once she settled primly in the witness chair, Greg Harlan walked her through the report of her findings as she had done hundreds of times before in her thirty-plus years working for the state.

Noah didn't object a single time, just let the respected doctor summarize without interruption as their team had intentionally planned.

Greg had her paint a picture of Brian's death, grisly enough details that a few members of the jury flinched exactly as he'd intended. Even then, Noah remained silent, allowing the portrayal of the body's gruesome appearance.

Smirking at the defense team, Greg passed his witness over.

If only Greg knew the approach Noah planned…

Troy managed to sit still—barely. Greg Harlan needed to be taken down a notch, and Silas's Chávez had been the man for the job.

While the information about Detective Marsh had supposedly been wiped from the record, unearthing evidence against the man's character hadn't unsettled the assistant DA as much as Troy and Noah would have liked.

At least Greg's reddened face had suggested their discrediting his witness had caught him by surprise.

But what Noah had planned for the medical examiner?

Even better.

With a kind smile, Noah stood and approached

the witness stand. "Dr. Loveling, your testimony was detailed and professional as always. But just so you know, I did tell the prosecution team prior to today that we didn't dispute any of the facts of Brian Parsons's death."

Dr. Loveling simply stared at Noah as though carved from stone.

"With that information, can you tell us why you think you've been called as a witness for the prosecution?"

"Objection," Greg called out loudly, rolling his eyes. "He's asking for speculation."

"Let me rephrase," Noah stated without taking his focus off the doctor. "If the defense team does not argue the facts of Mr. Parsons's death, then what is the purpose of your testimony?"

"Objection!" Greg's raised voice revealed his irritation.

"Sustained," the judge said.

"Withdrawn," Noah all but purred, having stated what he'd needed to.

Again, Troy fought off a grin.

"Dr. Loveling," Noah continued without missing a beat, "is there any information you gathered that disproves Mr. Barlowe's claims of self-defense?"

"No."

Giddiness rose inside Troy.

"Did your findings include any physical, *concrete*

evidence that proves he is guilty of first-degree murder?"

The doctor glanced at the prosecution team before answering with a clipped "No."

Troy had to bite his lip to keep from smiling.

Noah let the judge know he was done with the witness and returned to his chair.

Greg Harlan didn't bother with further questions, and the judge adjourned until two for lunch.

Murmurs broke out once the door closed behind the judge, and Troy gathered up their paperwork, his focus on the man moving in his periphery.

The three filed out of the courtroom along with Grace, and they all made their way past lingering reporters to a small restaurant within walking distance. Noah led their group, Silas at his side, and Troy couldn't keep his gaze off Silas's flexing ass as the two men ahead of him spoke quietly to one another.

He'd rather Silas had been by his side, clinging to his hand as though needing assurance that everything was going to be okay.

But Troy couldn't give him that. Not for their relationship—or their future depending on the jury.

He might never get a chance to—

"He likes you," Grace whispered, threading her arm through Troy's.

He yanked his focus off Silas and the thought of never getting a chance to top the curious kitty.

Although a bit pale, tiredness lining her eyes, Grace's smile appeared radiant. "Nothing my brother does surprises me, but you…" Grace pursed her lips, but the smile remained as she tilted her head. "I never knew he was attracted to men."

The thought of Silas checking out another guy burned his gut with jealousy, but he wouldn't. "He's not."

"Just you?"

Troy shrugged, heat rising to his face. He wasn't about to tell Silas's sister he definitely liked Troy's dick, trying new things, expanding his horizons—and seeming to enjoy the hell out of their every encounter.

"I think you're good for him."

Troy damn near tripped. "W-why do you think that?"

"He's calmer since you came into his life. Less…cagey."

"Cagey?" Troy echoed, needing clarification.

She snickered, her attention flitting toward her brother. "He doesn't like to be tied down, but I'm sure you're already aware of his reputation."

"I've heard a thing or two," Troy stated quietly, jealousy once more rousing.

"But you don't have to worry." Grace squeezed his arm, bumping him with her shoulder. "He watches you like I've never seen him look at anyone. Ever."

Longing, hope, and pain swirled together in Troy's stomach, making for a toxic brew of excitement and anxiety that weakened his knees. "And how's that?" He couldn't help but fish out her thoughts.

"Like he would move mountains to make you happy—keep you safe."

Troy swallowed hard at the truth she spoke.

His heart ached to convince his mind that honesty in all things might not be as important as he'd always held to.

19

Silas

Aforensics expert took the stand after lunch, but like the medical examiner, all the evidence of a physical fight and blood splatter…none of it could prove Silas wasn't acting in self-defense.

Silas rested easier in his chair, regardless of his consciousness of the delicious man beside him, but he knew the case against him was far from buttoned up. One man still lay between him and his own time in the stand.

And thank fuck Chávez had gotten what his team needed that morning and handed over the findings while they'd been on lunch break.

David Parsons, Brian's older brother, got sworn in next, glowering at Silas with hatred in his eyes. Like Detective Marsh, he spewed bullshit about Silas's character to paint him in a bad light. His use of the word fuck earned a nice request from the judge to refrain from speaking vulgarity in his courtroom.

The second time he dropped the F-bomb a few minutes later, the judge threatened to hold him in contempt.

Silas swallowed his grin and the snicker in his throat.

The man on the stand was a ticking time bomb with a level of crazy in his eyes that pinged suspicions in the back of Silas's brain. Could he have been the one trying to kill Silas, the one who'd put Troy in harm's way?

Silas would have to sic Chávez on his ass for further investigation—then hand that information over to the police since they hadn't gotten any leads.

Three times throughout the man's ramblings in response to Greg's questioning, Noah had to tear himself from disinterestedly fiddling with papers in front of him to toss out objections.

It took a stern warning from the judge to keep the angry, grieving witness on track.

"Would you please explain the relationship between your brother and Miss Barlowe?" Greg requested, veering David off the topic of Silas.

In Silas's periphery, Noah still didn't seem to pay attention as though David's testimony meant jack shit.

Neither did Troy on his other side.

The team had prepared for the information about to be shared, and while it might raise flags or possible questions as to Silas's claims, there just wasn't the evidence to back up the charges.

That didn't keep David from glaring at Silas, loathing in his stare. "She dumped him—two days prior to my brother's murder."

"Objection," Noah tossed out yet again over terminology used once before, but David corrected himself before the judge could speak.

"*Death*." He spat the word out like it poisoned his tongue. "My baby brother was devastated. Heartbroken. He wasn't angry or heading over there to hurt her. Brian got a text from an unknown number telling him to come get his shit out of her house that morning. He went with high hopes to win her back. So what if he had a gun? He carries that damn thing —*carried* it everywhere."

Greg handed over evidence of phone records showing the call from a burner phone, and even though David ranted a bit longer, his voice unsteady, he had nothing worthwhile to add.

"Mr. Parsons." Noah started his cross-examination from where he still sat, seemingly more interested in the files before him than the man on the stand. "Did you read the message between your brother and whoever purchased the untraceable number?"

The detectives hadn't been able to track down the owner of the burner phone.

"Nah—but he tells me everything. I offered to go with him—wish like hell I had." Yet another glare landed on Silas's face as Noah finally stood, approaching the stand.

"And are you in possession of Brian's cell phone?" Noah asked even though both parties knew the answer.

"It wasn't with his personal belongings when I picked them up from the morgue. Wasn't in Brian's car, either. When I call, it goes straight to fucking voicemail."

"Mr. Parsons!" The judge finally seemed to have enough and shot the man a glare of his own.

Troy tensed—and Silas bit back another chuckle.

"Sorry, Your Honor," David grumbled.

"Final warning: One more vulgar word, and I *will* hold you in contempt."

"Yes, Your Honor."

"Please continue," the judge told Noah and pressed his lips in a firm line.

"Do you have a screenshot of your brother's conversation with whoever was behind this unknown number?" Noah asked.

David slouched, crossing his arms. "Why the hell would I have that when I didn't even see the fu— " He cut off the word about to leave his lips. "Message?"

Noah nodded as though deep in thought, returning to the table to retrieve another piece of evidence. He ambled back toward David as though on a Sunday stroll, flipping through the pages, his squeaky shoe and flicking of paper loud in the heavy silence over the court.

Warmth and energy continued to radiate between Silas and Troy regardless of the walls the younger man had raised. Silas knew Troy protected his heart, and Silas hoped he would have the chance to ease his anxiety and answer whatever questions he might have.

He'd decided on honesty between them.

He just needed the chance to prove himself.

And the shit about to hit the fan for David Parsons would hopefully put him one step closer to freedom.

"Tell us about your relationship with Jose Garcia," Noah said, finally giving the man his full focus.

David, like Detective Marsh had done, paled, but he held Noah's stare. A pin could have dropped and sounded like thunder in the complete stillness hovering over those in attendance. No scuffling of feet, no whisper of breath at the drug runner's name coming up again within a matter of hours—and with two different witnesses.

"Cat got your tongue, Mr. Parsons?" Noah asked, his tone hinting at teasing.

David's chin lifted, his focus shifting off to the left. "Don't know the man."

"Hmm." Noah flipped through the papers again. "Court records that landed on my desk over the lunch break show otherwise. You've had a handful of charges brought against you for various petty crimes, but it was the heroin found on you that landed you behind bars a few years back."

"So?"

"So…" Noah once more gave his attention to David. "We're to believe a convicted felon's word without any sort of physical evidence to back your claims? Perhaps it was one of Garcia's other drug runners that put through a call. Perhaps it was the man himself."

David's face went red. "Are you saying my brother sold drugs for Garcia?"

"No—I'm telling the court that you took the blame for that heroin to keep your little brother out of trouble. That's the deal you made with Detective Marsh…correct?"

"What's your point?" David snipped, his face still flushed, but the judge let it go.

"The point being," Noah stated firmly, a smirk on his lips when Greg Harlan didn't bother with an objection, "the records show over a dozen different burner cell numbers contacted your brother's phone in the last thirty days alone—a total of fifty-seven calls, two of which went through around the same time the day before his death. You might have gone to jail to protect Brian, but you weren't able to keep him from getting into further trouble, were you?"

Finally Greg tossed out an objection for speculation, but Noah withdrew his words. "No further questions, Your Honor," he stated simply and once more ambled across the courtroom to take his seat.

David Parsons left the stand without questioning from the assistant DA, but his lingering stares of hatred before passing from sight made a rare shiver slide down Silas's spine.

The man would definitely need watching.

20

Troy

"Come home with me."

The demand whispered against Troy's ear made him shiver as he gathered up Noah's paperwork from their table. He filled his lungs with the subtle scent of Silas's cologne, swallowed the rush of saliva coating his tongue, and shook his head even though the energy brushing over his skin enticed him to obey.

"Please, Troy," Silas begged. "Let me explain—I can't fucking take this distance between us. I—I don't feel comfortable with you so far away. I can't keep an eye on you. Protect you."

"Those acts of violence weren't meant for me," Troy said quietly without giving Silas his eyes. "Being close to you puts me in more danger than staying at my apartment." He didn't allow his tone to suggest he could be swayed or argued with, but Troy didn't stick around to give Silas the chance.

The man was persuasive as hell, making Troy want to toss all his moral codes straight into a toxic dump site. But he'd clung to his stance on honesty for so many years, and the hurt that had taken him to that point still clutched at his soul.

He couldn't find a way to free himself even though he wanted to.

Troy left without a backward glance and hated his stubbornness the second he shut himself into his lonely rented bedroom.

Troy lay on his bed and stripped out of his suit coat and tie, his shoes kicked off and flung a few feet inside his door. Had he been in Silas's room, his clothing would be neatly folded, his dress shoes tucked beneath the edge of Silas's king-sized bed.

Longing swept over him, settling as an ache in his heart and groin.

Eyes stinging, he stared at the ceiling, wondering what the hell was wrong with him. The trauma of his past had jaded him so deeply, made him suspicious as fuck even though Silas had proven his protective nature twice over.

He felt sure Silas had taken Brian Parsons out purposefully for hurting his sister—but there wouldn't be any concrete evidence to convict. Noah and the team defending Silas had seen and heard all the assistant DA had in hand to push for a conviction.

But even without that needed information to find Silas guilty, Silas *was* in Troy's mind.

Because Troy had seen Silas's frantic need to check him for injury. He'd seen the cold, hard glint in Silas's eyes when speaking to the detectives about the attempts on his life.

Silas Barlowe was an alpha male through and through—and he would do anything…*anything*…for those he cared about.

Troy should have stumbled away from thoughts of giving in to Silas like he'd done when leaving the courthouse. But Grace stating what she had while threading their arms together and showing her acceptance of him in her brother's life only swayed his heart closer.

"Goddamnit." Troy rolled and grabbed his cell, swallowing hard to keep tears from spilling. "Talk to me, Chase," he blurted when his friend answered. "Tell me about that Gorgeous Goliath of yours that you love to climb like a tree."

"He let me have his ass last night."

"Oh God." Troy choked on a sob and curled into a ball. "I want it all. Every detail. Please."

"Are you okay?" Chase asked, his voice full of concern.

"No. I'm in love with a liar, a man on trial for killing a man in what he claims is self-defense."

"Shh."

"I know." Troy's attempt to stop his tears failed. "I'm not supposed to talk about the case, but…I just can't, Chase. Can't stop thinking about him, how he makes me feel. Can't stop wanting him—his hands, his mouth, his dick—his affection and words of praise when I please him."

"Oh, Troy." Chase let out a giggle, but Troy didn't take offense at his best friend's amusement. "You're good and truly fucked, aren't you?"

"Shut up."

"You'll never live your best life if you don't take chances."

"I can't."

"You can. Just give that man your full attention and fuck that shit from your past trying to keep you down. What if Silas is it for you? What if he's your forever man? The one who will love you until your last breath? The peanut butter to your jelly, the—"

"I'm not a romantic," Troy grumbled, cutting Chase short and causing him to snort.

"Negative Nancy. You need dick—*good* dick from someone who cares about more than just your greedy hole."

Troy actually chuckled and swiped at the wetness on his cheeks. He imagined the sparkle in Chase's eyes. Could see him two-stepping with silliness.

"Get some, then enjoy the love, life, and joy in store or you."

"Fuck, you've found a good therapist down there in Philly, haven't you?" Happiness welled inside Troy for his best friend.

"Yep. Angie take two—Delores is my new therapist—she's my person. Well, my *other* person. Drew Michael is my first. My one and only."

It was Troy's turn to snort. "Hardly your *only*."

"From here on out, he is," Chase argued, his tone full of sass. "And we don't focus on our past. We look to the future, to all it has in store for us. Neither of us would survive living in the shit of what came before—and I fear you won't either. Give it up, Troy. Grab life by the balls. Holler a 'Gimme!' and take what you want."

"I think he had something to do with Lennon's death too," Troy said, ripping the conversation back to serious with one sentence.

For the first time since Troy had met Chase, his best friend didn't have an instantaneous reply. Troy went on to tell him about the sticky note he'd seen and Silas's suspicious word choice when denying involvement.

"Perhaps…" Chase started after a brief silence, "learning the truth behind Silas's actions would help put your uptight-assed mind at ease. While on the verge of not being morally right, maybe he had your best interest in mind. If you ask me, he took a step out of love—and loving someone isn't a crime…so why would protecting that person be one?"

Lennon's death had satisfied a part of Troy's deepest thoughts that hadn't ever been put to rest. Did it truly matter how his rapist had met his end or what had enticed him to wrap a rope around his neck and kick the stool from beneath his feet?

Silas definitely hadn't made the killing blow, but even if he had, it would have been because of his deep feelings for Troy. An execution of justice the vigilante way since a guilty man had walked free.

Gray…so goddamn gray in a world Troy had seen as black and white for too long.

"You always make me feel better," Troy said on a sigh, stretching out once more and breathing a little easier.

"That's what my GG says," Chase said with a joking tone, probably winking.

Troy chuckled again, but his smile fell once he got off the phone with his best friend. Another day of court lay in the near future and a deliberation that would result in Silas either walking free or facing time behind bars.

Inaccessible to Troy, put away for years.

He should have been anxious to spend every possible second with Silas in the event the jury decided him guilty of the charges, but his heart already hurt enough.

A heavy sigh wilted Troy into his bed as he accepted the truth that one more night in Silas's arms would make the agony of separation that much worse.

He would hold his silence until the end. There was no point in getting his hopes up if there *wasn't* hope for a future together.

21

Silas

Silas took the stand, his stomach hard as rock, his emotions locked up tight. He hadn't slept worth a shit thinking about Troy and where his head was in regards to them—if there was a them anymore to even worry over.

Acid ate at his guts, twisting his insides into a frustrating knot of worry.

But his face stayed unlined and calm as always. Unmoved from its placid state as though untouchable—unaffected—by the situation he faced.

He rested in the witness chair regardless of his inner turmoil as Greg Harlan stood before him.

The assistant DA asked questions about the morning of Brian Parsons's death at a rapid rate, exactly as Noah and Troy had warned, but Silas stayed true to his story. Nothing Greg spewed or tossed out would make Silas change what he'd recounted countless times before.

His innocence.

Self-defense.

Then Greg brought back up that first piece of suspicious evidence that was too circumstantial to convict but could possibly cause doubt in jurors' minds—and definitely create an emotional mess between Silas and his sister.

"Please tell us who installed your sister's security system."

Silas didn't hesitate, didn't blink or inhale to fill his lungs wanting to seize over. "I did."

"And who all has access to turn the cameras off?"

"Me."

"Only you?" Greg asked for clarity.

"That is correct," Silas stated with a firm nod.

"And would you please tell the court why those cameras just happened to be shut down on the morning Brian Parsons came to visit your sister."

Silas refused to allow the prosecuting attorney's words to crawl beneath his skin. He fought the need to clench his jaw. It was time to spill the truth that could very well rip his independent sister from his life.

"My sister Grace is all the family I have left. She is the only person who has stood beside me since our parents' death years ago. As the big brother, I see her safety as my responsibility. She is mine to protect."

Silas filled his lungs quietly, without any hint of drama over the roiling of his insides.

"Once a month, I turn off her security cameras and let myself into her house after she leaves for work in order to check in on her life and lifestyle without her knowledge."

A whispered curse from behind the defense team rose.

Grace, no doubt.

"I planned on doing so once I finished up fixing her leaking drain," Silas stated.

He could feel Grace's anger. She hid her kinks from him because she didn't trust him with how she sought out her release. Grace, the precious little sister he watched after closer than anyone, enjoyed pain with her pleasure.

And unfortunately for Brian Parsons, he hadn't known where to draw the line between the two.

But the jury and those in the courtroom didn't need to heart *that* truth.

"So you went behind her back. Snooped through her private affairs, through her personal things," Greg asked.

"I did," Silas answered without hesitation.

"The fuck?" a voice growled—definitely Grace.

"Silence in the courtroom," the judge rebuked.

"Were you aware of Brian Parsons and your sister's relationship?" Greg asked Silas.

"No, I was not."

"But surely you saw them on her security cameras. You knew who it was that walked into Grace's house that morning."

"I never watched her—them—or him while in her home. Our relationships remaining private was something she and I agreed upon years ago. The video system is there for Grace to keep an eye on. I just get notifications of her alarm being activated and shut off."

The assistant DA's eyes blazed with frustration since there was no way to prove Silas lied. "How far would you go to protect your little sister, Mr. Barlowe?"

"There isn't anything I wouldn't do for Grace," Silas answered truthfully.

"Would you intentionally antagonize and lure in a man she had told you wouldn't leave her alone after the breakup?"

"No—like I said, I didn't find out about her dating him until the weekend after the attack when the press released his name and the truth of their relationship. Brian Parsons showed up unannounced at Grace's house, his intent clear by that gun in his hand," Silas continued, ready to set the asshole straight so they could move the fuck on. "He attacked, and I fought as any human would instinctively do when facing death. Yes, I'll admit to taking his life, but it was done as a last resort and with the sole intention to save my own."

Noah stood before Silas a few minutes later once Greg finished, his gaze steady. Sure and confident.

Silas was beginning to feel the same, and hope for fixing the two most important relationships in his life kept him focused on what he needed to say, all that Noah had coached him on.

"Tell us about the death of your parents."

"Objection!" Greg spouted off, grasping at straws because he understood he would be going down and not in a blaze of glory. "The death of Mr. and Mrs. Barlowe bear no weight in this case."

"I beg to differ," Noah argued, turning to face the judge. "Knowing Silas Barlow's past, learning the why of his reasons for being sometimes overly protective will shed light on his character, his ability to make good choices."

"Overruled," the judge responded to the prosecutions argument. "Continue."

"Silas?" Noah said, once more turning toward him.

Silas focused on Troy who sat chewing on his lower lip—bless the kid's heart, he bled empathy and longing even while trying to keep those fucking walls in place. A criminal defense attorney he would never be—without training from someone who could put on and hold a poker face.

Given the chance, Silas would be up to the task of teaching him.

He shifted his focus on his seething sister, shutting himself off from the pain and anger in her dark eyes from learning about his snooping.

"Our parents were ripped from our lives." Silas began the story of losing the ones he'd needed the most right out of college and learning the family business. They'd been taken too early in a tragic plane crash, leaving him and his baby sister orphaned. While he'd been twenty-five, well on his way to being a responsible adult, Grace had just turned nineteen, and a young one at that.

Forcing a bit of emotion to bleed through his voice he definitely didn't feel—or ever had, Silas conveyed what he and Grace had gone through. Their loss, resulting grief, and agonizing heartache.

And Grace knew as well as he did that he lied under oath.

Their parents hadn't ever been there for them. It had been Silas and Grace against the world.

And Silas would drop even more dishonest words to ensure he would be able to have her back in the future. The stretched tales about to fall from Silas's lips were simply an exaggeration of their past.

Silas braced his heart before spilling the bullshit tale of her teenage years, the nonexistent rebellious stage she'd gone through before settling down to become a veterinarian. Although a legal adult, he explained, Grace had needed someone to watch over her, protect her from poor choices. She'd made more than Silas had been able to stop from happening, he claimed, but he'd always been there to help her pick up the pieces.

And he would continue to do so…if she allowed it after his deception.

The faded anger, the dawning of realization smoothing out Grace's features suggested he would find forgiveness.

Eventually.

He didn't allow any outward expression even though he breathed easier.

One down, one to go…

"I'm a protective, possessive bastard by nature," Silas stated, finally removing his focus off his little sister.

His gaze collided with Troy's who watched him with longing in those gorgeous blue eyes. He swallowed, and Silas zeroed in on the action, his tongue remembering the delicious flavor of Troy's skin.

Would he have the chance to worship his lover again? Lose himself in the sweetest boy he'd ever met?

"What can I say?" Silas asked as his voice broke, showing rare vulnerability to all the people in the courtroom. "There's nothing I wouldn't do for the few people I love. Those who've proven themselves time and again." He stared pointedly at Troy, hoping the young man knew the words were meant for him. "If that means snooping, doing stuff behind a loved one's back to ensure their safety, I won't hesitate. Yes, I turned off those cameras that could have recorded the incident and proven my innocence beyond a shadow of a doubt. But given the choice again, I would do it all over in the hopes Brian Parsons would have changed his mind. That he would have stayed home that morning rather than trying to exact revenge over a broken heart."

A pin dropped to the floor could have shattered the silence, and Silas prayed to any god who might be listening that his heart wouldn't be the thing breaking.

The prosecution team didn't follow up with more questions, and the judge excused Silas.

He settled back beside Troy, inner tremors of need tempting him to wrap the kid in his arms. Breathe in his sweet, soothing scent. Bask in his soft hands running through Silas's hair.

He yearned for affirmation in that moment more than the oxygen he fought to fill his lungs with.

Because Silas had fallen hard and fast. Truly. Honestly. And he wanted a future with the elfin angel who'd caught up his soul with a death grip so hard that he longed to submit to its rest.

But they weren't yet done with proving his innocence.

22

Troy

Having called their last witness, the prosecution rested, but Troy felt far from relieved.

His body hummed with electrical energy radiating off Silas beside him. The scent of him and the heat of his body reached for Troy as though a tangible force, enticing him to give in.

To lust, to the possibility of love. To a future.

Troy longed to take life by the balls like both his mom and Chase had pushed him to do. He wanted the same happiness inflected in his best friend's voice when speaking about the person he'd found —*his* person.

No perfect man existed, no one sitting on a high horse, honest in all things.

Was Troy willing to set aside his ridiculous standards and believe in the one who he knew would do anything for him?

There was no doubt Silas would even sacrifice himself. He'd protected Troy with his own body—twice—and he'd openly declared his feelings for Troy to everyone in that courtroom paying attention.

Silas loved him. Desperately. Dearly.

And Troy longed to accept all he offered, all he had to give—even if it wasn't the perfection he'd aways thought he'd wanted.

Every man had flaws, and if loving to the point of exacting revenge like a vigilante outlaw was Silas's, then at least Troy would always be assured of his safety.

It was the defense's team to shine, and Troy forced himself to focus on the task at hand. He couldn't fail in being a solid team member ready to fight for Silas's freedom.

Because in that moment, he made his decision.

Silas had barreled into his life uninvited, and guilty or innocent, Troy had no wish for him to be ripped away as Silas and Grace's parents had been.

While Troy knew some of what Silas had claimed under oath stretched truth about his and Grace's lives after their parents deaths—he'd definitely crossed into gray territory with that little tale—he understood Silas's reasons for doing so.

Love for his sister.

Love for *him*.

Being behind bars and away from both of them would drive Silas insane, slowly kill him, same as it would to Troy.

Straightening in his chair, attempting to wipe emotion from his face, Troy turned toward Noah and nodded, ready to help protect the man he loved.

His boss winked, clasped Silas's shoulder beside him, and stood. "The defense calls Javier Chávez to the stand," he stated, and the man Troy had worked closely with the previous couple of weeks walked the short aisle through the gallery to stand before the judge and swear to speak the truth.

The prosecution team had already lost their attempts to get the information thrown out that the private investigator would testify to.

Troy had seen the evidence Chávez had gathered. Read the concrete findings that couldn't be disputed. While there was no video proof of Silas's innocence, the words in black and white legal documents would more than create a shadow of doubt in any sane juror's mind about Brian Parsons's intent that morning.

"Would you please state your name and occupation for the jury?" Noah began, allowing the private investigator to prove his professionalism and worthiness to bear witness in Silas's defense.

A few of the jury members nodded their acceptance at hearing Chávez's credentials, which included time in the Marines, and Troy smothered the smile wanting to stretch his lips. His skin buzzed, and he forced himself to remain still as the investigator began answering Noah's questions about what he'd uncovered concerning Brian Parsons.

"Objection!" Greg called out within seconds of Chávez beginning to speak. "The deceased isn't on trial."

"I'm painting a picture of Brian Parsons's volatility," Noah explained what Greg was already aware of. The poor bastard was simply grasping at straws. "The reason Silas Barlowe would fear for his life."

"I'll allow the questioning—for now," the judge replied, "but no theatrics. No drama."

"Of course, Your Honor," Noah agreed and turned back toward Chávez. "Please continue with your findings."

"Two years ago, Brian Parsons assaulted his estranged wife, Mandy Cleavers-Parsons. She laid in the ICU for three days before the doctors realized she would win the fight for a future."

The private investigator scanned the jurors' faces with grave, dark eyes, pausing on each one at a time until they grew restless beneath his steady stare.

He went on to explain about the second woman

to break Brian's heart that he had beaten to within an inch of her life. She eventually recovered even though she'd already lingered on the edge of fading away due to heavy drug use.

Brian Parsons had been convicted of breaking and entering that woman's house, but he'd escaped prosecution for attempted murder—because of a payoff outside court to protect the junkie's rich family from unsavory media spotlight over the shit their daughter had been into.

Twice more he'd been charged with physical assault, and both times he'd been let off the hook with nothing more than a slap on the wrist.

Brian Parsons's past unfolded in horrific details and more than suggested a believable reason he'd shown up at Grace's home that morning—with intent to inflict bodily harm for that broken heart his brother had claimed he suffered from.

The assistant DA along with his two team members sitting before the judge visibly paled with every bit of information leaving Chávez's mouth. They'd obviously put too much faith in their ability to get the evidence tossed out or in objecting successfully to the line of questioning, but there was nothing they could say to keep the truth of Brian Parsons's nature from the jury.

While Noah could have unleashed hell the day before when Detective Marsh and David Parsons had been on the stand, he'd saved the aces he'd kept up his sleeve as a final gavel smash, resting the case with sure thunder.

When Chávez finished outlining Brian Parsons's true persona, the one hidden by bribes and shady dealings to keep his record supposedly clean, Noah moved toward the defense's table. He didn't smile. Didn't smirk. Didn't show one trace of satisfaction or the emotions a man would feel knowing he stood on the verge of victory.

Noah had already been on a pedestal in Troy's mind, but in that moment, his admiration for his boss, the son of the man who'd taken but lost Troy's case, grew tenfold.

But unlike his father who'd believed and fought for justice for Troy to the end, Noah would win.

There was no doubt.

Troy offered Noah the final bit of evidence that *had* to bring easy conclusion to the juror's minds if they hadn't already swayed toward a verdict of innocent.

Noah presented the paperwork to the judge, offering its numbered label before handing a copy to the assistant DA. He then turned to those who held Silas's future in their hands. "Chávez, will you please tell the jury how you came about the documentation of all your findings concerning Brian Parsons, please?"

"Boston's Chief of Police."

A gasp sounded from somewhere behind Troy, and he felt delicious stirrings of satisfaction curling like glorious morning fog inside him. He wasn't able to withhold the happiness from lifting his lips.

What the jury went on to learn was Chávez's friendship with Detective Marsh's boss. The two men had grown up on the streets together, having one another's backs even after they had dragged themselves from the slums of Roxbury.

And at Chávez's suggestion, the chief had dug into the shady dealings, hidden files uncovered— both about Detective Marsh and Brian Parsons.

What Chávez didn't share was that a certain drug runner—Garcia—was also in good with Chávez whose pockets ran deep thanks to his client, Silas Barlowe. It had been Garcia's greased hands that enticed the unsavory man to spill the beans on Parsons and Marsh and all the shit they'd managed to hide from Boston's PD.

At the raised eyebrows, thinned lips, and glances of the jury members at one another concerning all the coverups, Troy's smile widened.

No warrant for the detective's arrest had yet been issued, but he would have his day in court—and would be found guilty as fuck.

Closing arguments lasted less than five minutes each.

Deliberation only an hour longer.

Silas Barlowe was cleared of all charges in the death of Brian Parsons.

Elation choked the oxygen from Troy's lungs. Tears hazed his eyes. And he cursed his inability to hide the emotions from his face as court adjourned.

Silas and Noah shared a bro-hug, and Troy stood trembling, waiting for Silas to turn toward him.

"You fucking bastard," Grace hissed from directly behind them, drawing her brother's attention off Noah. "What the fuck, Silas? Snooping through my shit? Seriously?" Face red and lips in a thin line, she glowered at her brother, arms wrapped tight around her middle.

Silas's shoulders didn't sag, and he didn't visibly wilt beneath her anger, the fallout Troy knew he'd expected from his sister.

"Grace…" Noah stated her name quietly, firmly, and she blinked.

Tearing her focus off Silas, she looked at Noah… and took a shuddering breath.

Troy glanced between the two of them, same as Silas did as unspoken words seemed to pass through the air separating the attorney and Silas's sister.

A few seconds ticked past in tense silence before Grace moved her focus back on Silas, chin lifting— as though Noah had subdued her without more than speaking her name. "We'll talk later."

Silas nodded.

She turned away to gather her things—and Silas finally, *finally*, gave Troy his full attention.

A shiver pebbled the skin on Troy's arms hidden beneath his suit, and he swallowed hard at the clear question in Silas's eyes.

"Yeah," Troy whispered, his eyes welling.

Silas let out a heavy exhale, hands twitching at his sides. The first physical evidence of emotion since the trial had begun. "Later," he promised quietly, his tone haggard and sexy as hell.

Troy couldn't find his voice, so he simply nodded.

Outside, the sun shone bright, high in the sky. Warmth slid over Troy's face, similar to the heat of anticipation inside him.

Reporters closed in on their team—Noah and Silas in the lead, Troy and Grace following as usual. Questions rang out, and as Noah came to a standstill to offer comments, a flash of quick movement in Troy's periphery drew his attention.

David Parsons slipped between the crowd, his lips in a grim line. Hardened eyes focused on Silas.

Murder rested in those depths—

Without thought, Troy moved forward as Parsons's arm raised. A Glock came into sight—and Troy jumped in front of Silas.

"No!" The word ripped from his lungs, less than a whisper—he needed time. A chance to make things right—to say the words he longed to hear in return.

An explosive blast rang in his ears.

Pain ripped through his chest and stole his breath.

Chaos erupted but faded as quickly as it had begun.

Darkness swallowed Troy into nothingness.

23

Silas

Silas paced across the emergency department's waiting room, his stomach in knots and Troy's—fuck, his precious lover's blood soaked through and dried on his shirt. Rage continued to tear through him, making it hard to see the path he'd strode dozens of times already.

Troy lay in surgery.

He hadn't opened his eyes, hadn't uttered a single word after throwing himself into harm's way to save Silas. Not one flicker of his eyelids or twitch of muscle assured Silas as he'd clutched Troy to his chest, bellowing for someone to help him.

His first instinct had been to save Troy in return, but he'd been powerless to do more than leak tears from his eyes, pleading for him to be okay while cops wrestled David Parsons to the ground.

Silas hadn't given the man a second thought until

they'd arrived at the hospital and Troy passed from his sight into the ER.

Murderous emotions choked him.

The need to rip apart the man who'd shot his boy caused his hands to flex at his sides.

His shoulders hunched, a hard grimace on his face.

Noah and Grace sat beside one another in silence, having been barked at a few times for their attempts to calm Silas.

Their glances at one another gave themselves away—but one of Silas's connections down in Rhode Island had already made him aware of their affair. He'd kept his silence about where the two of them went to unwind and would continue to do so, but only because he trusted Noah to take care of his sister.

Noah would be good for her. He would draw her from behind the walls she'd erected in the same manner Silas had.

They would have each other, but what about him?

Silas had finally found the one person he wanted to share everything with, and Silas didn't know if he still breathed…if he drew oxygen into his lungs on his own…if his heart still beat.

Agony slashed through his chest like a hot knife, and Silas paused in his pacing, eyes closing. He couldn't inhale deeply enough, couldn't—

"Silas."

"Don't," he ordered at Grace through clenched teeth. He didn't want to hear assurances she couldn't offer. Didn't want her arms around him. Didn't want any physical touch that wasn't Troy's. "Fuck." Silas swallowed hard and tipped his head back, fighting off the desire to roar his anger and frustration, the pain tearing his insides apart.

Love was one lethal, motherfucking bitch…

"Mr. Barlowe?"

Silas's eyelids shot open, and he spun.

The surgeon approached, his face a mask of indifference, similar to the one Silas donned every goddamn day.

"Troy?" Silas choked out the name, his heart cold in his chest.

"Out of surgery, stable, and resting."

"Thank fuck." Silas's breath left in a rush, his body sagging beneath the release of adrenaline's choke hold the previous couple of hours.

The surgeon went on to explain how the bullet miraculously hadn't hit Troy's lung. A few centimeters to the right and he might not have made it.

"When can I see him?" Silas asked, his voice nothing but rasp and need.

"I can have one of the nurses take you back shortly. He's still sedated but ought to be waking soon."

A few words of thanks from Silas, and the surgeon left.

Silas sank into the chair beside Grace, elbows on knees and head hanging low. He didn't pull away from her as she hugged his back, but he soaked in the comfort she offered.

They hadn't spoken about the actions he'd taken to keep her safe, something they would need to do to clear the air between them, but her support let him know they would get over his deviousness.

The look in Troy's eyes, the simple "Yeah" he'd whispered had given Silas hope that they too would be okay. Troy didn't like shades of gray in his black and white world, but somehow he'd come to accept Silas as-is.

Silas rubbed hands down over his face, heaving another heavy exhale that sagged him further into the hard chair.

"Will you take her home for me?" he asked Noah without lifting his focus off the floor beneath his blood-splattered dress shoes.

"Of course."

"Silas?" Grace asked, withdrawing her body from against his but resting a hand on his shoulder.

"I'll be fine—as long as Troy is, I will be."

Noah and Grace shifted in his periphery, readying to leave.

"Call me if you need me," Grace whispered and kissed the top of Silas's downturned head.

"I will," Silas choked out, his relief over his sister's continued love and loyalty stirring additional emotions into his already overwhelmed head and heart.

She would always have his back, same as he would hers.

No matter what.

No matter when.

"Noah!" Silas called, pushing to his feet before the two let him to his thoughts.

Grace glanced between the men as Silas approached them. He didn't stop until he crowded into Noah's personal space, using his intimidating presence like he did in every business transaction.

"Hurt her," Silas whispered, allowing Noah to see the cold, hard truth in his stare, "and I'll kill you."

Noah studied him in silence, a question rather than wariness in his eyes—but he didn't speak. Didn't ask.

Neither did Grace. Not a single noise rose from whatever emotions Silas's promise had roused inside her. Either she trusted Noah, or she knew beyond a shadow of a doubt that her big brother would do anything in his power to protect her.

Silas hoped it was both.

Noah dipped his head in understanding, and he turned away from Silas and the threat. His hand pressed in a possessive hold against Grace's back as he led her from the waiting room.

Left alone with his thoughts, Silas once more sank into a chair, closed his eyes, and offered up his first prayer *ever* of thankfulness to whatever saint or god might exist.

It was a couple hours before Troy became lucid enough for Silas's liking. He sat beside Troy's hospital bed, the steady beep of the machine hooked up to monitor his heart rate behind him.

Troy rested easy. Drugged up and pale, but no less beautiful.

Silas's chest burned at the sight of him breathing, those gorgeous blue eyes hazed by drugs studying his own. He clutched Troy's hand with both of his, leaning forward in the uncomfortable as fuck chair, pressed as close to the damn bed as he could be.

"I'm going to tell you everything," Silas whispered.

"No," Troy croaked the word, squeezing his fingers.

"I lied to you," Silas admitted.

"You simply…kept the truth from me in order to protect you and Grace…and what we have."

Hope rose again, same as it had when Troy had smiled at him after court had adjourned.

"Do we still have it?" Silas asked anyway, needing verbal assurance. "Because I've got to be honest with you, no one has ever had my back like you did today. Almost losing you…" Silas swallowed audibly as emotion once more swirled inside him like a goddamn nor'easter.

Troy didn't speak, simply studying Silas's face. An expression of pain and love Silas couldn't withstand poured from his lover's soul.

"Will you do the right, honorable thing and turn me in?" Silas whispered, fear still a very real demon inside his head.

"Double jeopardy," Troy rasped without hesitation, a slight smirk tilting his lips. "But even if the law allowed it, I need you too much to see you behind bars."

Silas choked out a laugh at the relief sweeping over him. "I'm a bad influence on you."

"You're the best thing that's ever happened to me," Troy argued, finally revealing a smile on his bee-stung lips Silas wanted to kiss, lick, and bite forever.

"You're moving into my place when you're released from here." Silas didn't bother with asking.

"What if I don't want to?"

"You do," Silas assured him and leaned forward, gently brushing his mouth over Troy's. "You just don't know it yet."

24

Silas

few weeks later...

Silas deactivated Grace's security cameras before letting himself into her home. She'd changed her locks and code, but she should have figured that wouldn't keep her big brother from invading her privacy.

He didn't need to snoop. He already had knowledge tucked away from good sources that revealed Noah could take care of her in the way she needed.

No, Silas trespassed for an entirely different reason.

Knowing she spent more time with Noah than in her own home, Silas didn't expect to find any evidence of the young attorney's presence in her personal space. Not that he was looking, but Grace tended toward a lack of good housekeeping skills, and it appeared that Noah did as well after their dinner date.

Her cleaning service also hadn't visited before Silas had arrived.

Silas bypassed the kitchen but noted two used wine glasses with remnants of red in the bottom on the counter beside the sink.

He meandered past the living room's entrance, unable to help noticing the black, lacy bra slung over the couch's cushion and the high heels also close by.

A pile of rumpled tissues sat on the coffee table—and a tied-off condom atop.

He wanted to growl at the thought of her sister's body being invaded by any man, but at least the fucker had taken consideration and sheathed that shit up.

Teeth clenched, Silas made for Grace's office and their father's massive desk at the room's center. The rolling chair squeaked as he settled into it, the bottom file drawer on the right stubborn as always and making a similar noise as the seat as Silas pulled it open.

He removed the files, taking care to keep them in order while piling them atop the desk—then pressed in the drawer's back bottom corner.

The secret compartment he'd found after his

parent's death had long since been emptied of damning paper evidence, the sort that would soil the Barlowe name and quite possibly rip the family business from Silas's grasp regardless of the connections and strength he'd gained over the years.

He'd learned where his ruthlessness came from, his love of walking the gray edge of morality.

Silas Barlowe was no more innocent than his father, but men did what they needed to in order to protect their family.

Even if it meant dealing with those on the wrong side of the law—mafia, drug lords, and biker gangs like the Vicious Vipers MC up on the North Shore.

Only one item lay in the secret hiding spot.

Silas lifted Brian Parsons's cell from the compartment and tucked it safely in the back pocket of his jeans. Knowing the slimy bastard as he had, Silas hadn't concerned himself that any tracking device would lead authorities to the missing phone that contained text messages between Parsons's and a burner phone long since destroyed.

Lips in a grim line, Silas replaced the compartment's hidden lid, leaving the space beneath empty. Files once more filled the drawer, and he pushed it closed with finality.

Carrying the one piece of concrete evidence that would have changed the outcome of Silas's trial, he exited the house. Locked it up behind him.

And turned Grace's security cameras back on.

Troy sat waiting in the driveway, Silas's car still running to keep the interior cool.

Silas slid back into the driver seat and released a heavy exhale.

"Did you get it?"

"I did," Silas told him and leaned over the console to take his lover's mouth in a heated kiss. He'd woken Troy two hours earlier by pressing his lubed dick into his tight hole he'd wrecked the night before—their first time after his release from the hospital.

Same as then, Silas swallowed down the whimpers on Troy's lips.

"You're a tease," Troy grumbled, breathless and needy when Silas pulled away.

"I was thinking we ought to head out on our new yacht for a week or two. Decompress now that you're completely healed. Maybe feed pieces of plastic and crushed electronics to the fishies."

Silas could feel Troy's gaze on his face as he backed out of his sister's driveway.

"Since I know you won't allow me to stay behind, I suppose I can join you."

Grabbing Troy's hand and holding it atop his thigh, Silas grinned, relaxed for the first time since learning Brian Parsons had been the one to blacken his sister's eye. "I'm a possessive, protective asshole," Silas told Troy, no ounce of regret in his voice.

"As if I need the reminder," Troy said, sass in his tone but a fuck ton of happiness too.

25

Troy

The yacht floated miles off the coast of Massachusetts, its gleaming deck and polished chrome railings shining beneath the full moon in the night sky.

But the beams of light couldn't breach what lay beneath, deep in the bowels of the ship where Troy stood before Silas, glossed lips parted and panting while Silas stripped him down.

Troy hadn't ever allowed Silas to fill him in on the details of what had led to either Parsons's or Lennon's death. He didn't care about the past and chose to focus on the future. Speaking of what had come before them would only keep the memories fresh in his mind when all he wanted to do was move forward.

Silas had told him a piece of evidence lay hidden inside his sister's house, and Troy hadn't been surprised by what it was, nor was he against burying it forever.

There had been forgiveness from Grace and Troy alike, and Silas once more seemed settled.

Less…cagey as his sister had called it.

Troy liked to think of it has incandescent happiness, wishes and dreams come true.

His had. He had Silas right where he wanted him.

In his arms, his heart—his future.

"I want your dick," Silas murmured, ghosting his mouth over Troy's, his hands busy shoving down his jeans.

"Then get on your knees," Troy sassed, his cock twitching in anticipation.

Silas pulled back, the intensity, the desire in his eyes flipping Troy's stomach. "In my ass, angel, not my mouth."

"Oh fuck." Troy grabbed hold of his length and squeezed, groaning at the thought of sinking into Silas's virgin hole.

"Can you give me that?"

"For all of maybe two seconds before blowing my load, yeah."

"As long as you're bare and filling me up, I don't care how fucking long you last. Just want to feel you, boy."

"Oh fuck," Troy repeated, trembling and wide eyed, too far gone in his lust to care about the term Silas still joked with.

Silas stepped back, slowly removing his clothing, teasing the ever loving shit out of Troy whose tongue salivated over rippled muscle and tanned skin. "See something you like?"

Troy's throat bobbed as he swallowed against his nerves. "Love."

Silas's focus jerked up from Troy's mouth to his eyes.

"*Love*," Troy whispered the word again, searching Silas's gaze.

They hadn't yet used the word to express the emotions that had only intensified since their first meeting, one brought about by lies, deceit, and murder.

But Troy no longer gave a shit about the gray lines Silas had traversed on a daily basis. He loved the man—his soul, his mind, just being with him. Moving into Silas's penthouse suite had been the best choice he'd made aside from submitting to his desire for the arrogant bastard.

"You love me." Silas didn't state it as a question as the corners of his lips curled upward, those damn hazel eyes of his lighting with more joy and contentment than Troy had ever seen.

"And you love me," Troy told him, assurance in his tone even though he shivered, fought off the shakes.

"I do." Silas hadn't hesitated to respond—and it

sounded too much like forever for Troy to keep his hands to himself.

Butterflies erupting in his belly, he launched at Silas, attacking his mouth, his hands frantic to touch, map out every inch he'd worshiped dozens of times since they'd met.

"Want you," he whispered, tilting his head for Silas to suck on his neck.

"Need you," his lover murmured back before licking up his neck and taking his lips in a kiss that consumed Troy's thoughts and pumped adrenaline through his system.

Silas was the one to tear away, and Troy once more had to grab hold of the base of his dick and squeeze. He watched Silas's ass flex with every step toward the bed.

Sprawled on his back, Silas crooked a finger.

Troy bit on the inside of his lip and obeyed, crawling between Silas's thighs as he spread them wide, knees near his chest.

"Silas…" Troy stared at his lover's drawn up balls, the smooth taint beneath, and the puckered hole with its dusting of black hair. "Fuck." He ran his fingertip over Silas's ass, groaning at the softness. "I'm not gonna last."

"Then you better hurry the fuck up because I want to feel you inside me, Mr. Emerson. I want you so fucking deep I can't breathe."

Their gazes caught and held as Silas patted

around the bed for the bottle of lube he'd tossed there earlier. "Get me ready."

Troy filled his lungs, steeled his resolve, and did as told.

At the first breach of his finger through Silas's ring of muscle, the older man grimaced and Troy hissed. Such tightness…heat.

"Want me to stop?" he croaked even though that was the last damn thing he wanted to do.

"No."

Troy bit his lip while feeling around the hot insides of Silas's hole, one untouched before him. Satisfaction swarmed through him, filling his chest with a possessiveness he'd never experienced before.

"You're mine," he stated, chin lifted while pressing in with a second finger.

Silas's erection flagged, but he groaned, lifting his knees higher. "Fucking right."

Troy took his time scissoring Silas's ass to a softened state, readying him to take Troy's dick. While not graced with the same girth as Silas, Troy would definitely push deeper into Silas's body than he did Troy's.

He bent over Silas's groin and sucked down his semi, determined to get him hard and leaking again. Troy didn't just want to own him. He wanted Silas to love having his hole stuffed full, hoped he would beg for it again in the future.

"Fuck…shit, baby. Fuck, yes." Silas swelled

against his tongue, his hips moving in time with the fingers fucking his ass. "Goddamnit, Troy. I need… fuck, give me more."

Troy worked in a third finger while tonguing Silas's slit and watching his face.

There was no hardening of features or a mask of indifference. Red fused Silas's cheeks. Lips parted, he panted. Eyes darkened by lust watched every move Troy made.

"Troy…"

Smirking around Silas's length, Troy backed away, popping off his dick. "Need something else in this tight hole?" Troy asked with sass in his voice. He curled his fingers, gliding over Silas's prostate.

"Shit!" Silas's back bowed, his eyes rolling upward. "Holy fucking shit…do that again."

Grinning, Troy took his lover to the brink, showing him how delicious being on the receiving end of a good prostate massage could be.

"Please, Troy…please."

Silas Barlowe begging for dick…

Shaking his head, his nerves calmed from focusing on the wrecked man before him, Troy stroked lube over his length.

He pressed in close, his hand on the bed beside Silas's thigh. Lining up the tip of his dick against Silas's puckered hole, he lifted his gaze. Lust-hazed eyes stared back at him, pupils overwhelming the hazel-green.

"I love you," Troy whispered and pushed forward.

"I lo—goddamn…fucking hell!" Silas gritted his teeth, and Troy paused, less than two inches inside the most exquisite, delicious heat he'd ever felt grasping at his cockhead.

Pausing, his heart expanding over the words Silas had been about to respond with, Troy gave him a few seconds to adapt to feeling a stiff dick invading his ass. Troy bit his own lip to keep from erupting—fucking bare. Inside Silas.

Luscious warmth. Beyond snug…fucking divine.

He couldn't think in full sentences.

Silas's body relaxed the slightest bit, and he released a heavy exhale.

"Okay?" Troy asked, his voice strangled.

"Yeah. Give me more."

Watching Silas closely, noting every wince, every muscle spasm in his jaw or flutter of his eyelashes, Troy worked his way in until their groins pressed tight. He was so close…so goddamn fucking close to losing it.

At least he'd gotten fully inside his lover's body.

"Talk to me, Silas," he whispered, needing to hear the words he lusted for more than the hot hole strangling his cock.

"Feels like I have a goddamn spear shoved up my ass," Silas stated through clenched teeth.

Troy barked out a laugh, the edge of his climax backing off the slightest bit. "Want me to stop?"

"Fuck no, my elfin angel—I want this. Want *you*. Make me feel good like only you can."

Troy shifted to plank over his lover, causing his length to move inside Silas. Troy took note of his blink, one that was a far cry from distaste or disgust.

He nipped Silas's lower lip and slowly dragged from his hot sheath, giving the man another taste of a stroking cock inside his body.

Silas cursed, and Troy grinned even though the base of his spine tingled. "Okay?"

"Fuck yeah." Silas dropped his hold on the backs of his knees and wrapped a heel around Troy's ass. "Now fuck me. Wreck me. Make me yours."

"Oh, baby...you're already mine," Troy teased, taking his time to slowly fuck in and out of Silas's body while Silas attempted to yank him back in faster. Harder. "You were mine the second I walked into that holding room all those months ago."

"Told you I was a sure thing," Silas stated with a gasp as Troy buried deep.

"Mmm," Troy agreed and laid on Silas with his full weight—and his full focus, fucking him in the way he wanted.

Hard. Deep enough he caught Silas's breath and made sexy as fuck groans rumble in his chest.

Troy's balls seized after only a handful of thrusts, and the noises spilling from Silas's lips, his encouragement for Troy to give him more, sent Troy over the edge.

"Fucking hell…sorry…fuck." Groaning, Troy emptied his balls inside Silas, but he didn't go lax. The second he finished, he scurried down Silas's body and swallowed his leaking dick, desperate to please his lover.

Shoving three fingers deep inside Silas, he sought out and located his prostate while his spunk dripped from his knuckles.

"Goddamnit…fuck!"

Silas bowed, his cum erupting into Troy's throat on the second stroke.

"Oh fuck…fucking *hell*," he moaned, head lifting to watch as Troy swallowed every spurt of his release. "God." Spent, Silas collapsed back, eyes closing.

Troy licked him clean and gently removed his fingers from Silas's body, wiping them on the rumpled sheets beside his hips. "Okay?"

"Fucking love you," Silas all but growled the words and yanked Troy atop his chest.

Their mouths fused, and Troy sank into the warm embrace, thankful as fuck he'd taken life by the balls, just like Chase had encouraged him to do.

He'd found his man, and nothing, no one, would ever separate them.

"Here, fishy, fishy," Silas called like one would to a child while tossing another tiny piece of plastic into the dark ocean far below.

Troy stood beside him along the top deck's railing, pressed against his side, studying his lover's face in the moonlight. "No more violence," he stated, dissolving Silas's rare, carefree, and absolutely gorgeous grin. "No retribution."

Lips thinning, Silas continued throwing the remnants of Brian Parsons's cell phone into the abyss where they would never be found. "I can't promise I won't gut someone if they try to harm you," he finally stated.

Troy knew without doubt that if David Parsons had escaped attempted manslaughter charges, he'd have been dead by Silas's hand within a matter of hours upon finding freedom.

"You're mine," Silas continued. "My love, my life…my family."

A shuddered inhale filled Troy's lungs as warmth spread through his entire body.

"We both know the lengths I'll go to save you from harm. It's instinctive, same as your jumping in front of that bullet meant for me. I can't stop it, and I refuse to allow hurt if I can keep it from happening."

Few pieces remained in Silas's palm, and Troy moved to wrap himself around him. He pressed his cheek against Silas's back, breathing in the scent of man, sex, and that cologne he would gladly drown in.

"Just…don't do anything stupid, okay?"

Silas snorted and turned, his hands empty until he gathered Troy against him, palms on his ass cheeks. "I'm always careful." He pecked Troy on the lips. "Thorough in hiding what needs to remain buried."

"I've relented on the whole honesty is always the best policy thing being wrong," Troy reminded him, "but no more violence. I mean it. Please."

Silas pressed a lingering kiss to the top of Troy's head, and Troy snuggled in close, knowing by Silas's gentleness and affection that he'd won that battle.

"I told you that first day I met you that I would give you anything you wanted," Silas murmured.

Troy tipped his head back and ran a fingertip over Silas's soft mouth. "I remember you saying something along the lines of you marking up my pale, pretty skin…thoroughly fucking me until my hair is a mess."

Silas dug his fingertips into Troy's ass, grinding his semi against him. "I do that every time I have you under me."

Troy snorted even though Silas spoke the truth.

"Still think my confidence is off-putting?" Silas asked, a sexy as fuck smirk twitching his mouth as he lowered his head, inches from Troy's face.

"You know I lied," Troy whispered, shivers racing over his skin.

Silas brushed his lips over Troy's. "Yeah, angel. I know. Now, what do you say we go below deck so I can worship your body until I wring every ounce of cum from those smooth balls I love to suck on?"

"Yes, please and thank you." A rush of love and longing swept over Troy, worth every gray line he'd crossed to be with Silas Barlowe.

THE END

Due Justice Duet continues with Due Diligence, Grace and Noah's story, written by Cecile Tellier.

About the Author

Lynn Burke is an international bestselling and award-winning author. A stay-at-home mom, she's a lover of coffee and vino, and with three spawn and two fur babies underfoot, noise levels dictate the daily switch-over time. In her few quiet 'me' moments, she can be found hunched over her Mac, trying to type as fast as her muse spews hot stories.

You can find more about Lynn at her website: www. authorlynnburke.com

Also By Lynn Burke

Abel's Obsession

Divulging Secrets

Healing Storms

In Between

Reluctant Lumberjack

Resisting his Mate

The Playboy Bachelor

Billion Dollar Love Anthology

Blood Born Series

Bonds of Worship Series

Dark Leopards MC

Darkest Desires Series

Devil's Outlaws MC

Elite Escort Series

Fallen Gliders MC

Forbidden Obsession Duet

Found by Fate Series

Midnight Sun Series

Missing Link Series

Risso Family Series

Sandy Ridge Series

Sinful Nature Series

Vicious Vipers MC

www.ingramcontent.com/pod-product-compliance
Lightning Source LLC
Chambersburg PA
CBHW070457200726
48293CB00007B/2259